James was born and raised in the surfing district of Australia's Sunshine Coast before moving to the Americas, where he studied Spanish literature and travelled extensively. Now back home, he draws on those experiences to engage his readers in stories of the human condition, and transports them to places he has come to know and love.

To the people in my life and the memories they have created
for me. I say thank you.

James McAlloon

DRAWN BY WATER

AUSTIN MACAULEY PUBLISHERS™

LONDON • CAMBRIDGE • NEW YORK • SHARJAH

A CIP catalogue record for this title is available from the British Library.

ISBN 9781528986007 (Paperback)
ISBN 9781528986014 (ePub e-book)

www.austinmacauley.com

First Published (2020)
Austin Macauley Publishers Ltd
25 Canada Square
Canary Wharf
London
E14 5LQ

Jan: Late nights, constructive feedback and unyielding support.

Chapter 1

My father often spoke of the dictatorship, and how his mixed emotions towards the actions of an imposed government made him feel like a traitor for leaving, guilty for abandoning his people but proud to have the courage to give his family a better life.

In some ways, he felt that he was running from himself. He spoke of his heritage, introduced Chilean culture and food into the home and told stories, which brought life back into the eyes of a true patriot just longing to go home. The Brazilians call it 'Saudade', the Welsh 'Hireath'. Dad called it 'Chile'.

I adored his passion and hoped to one day know the places he spoke of. As a girl, I would always question him, "When are we going to your home? When do I get to be a Chilean, Dad?" The interrogation didn't stop, until one day he became sick. For the following year, I would accompany him in silence to his weekly hospital visits, until one day he moved there fulltime. As my mum took off after my birth and I didn't have any other family, I was given permission to stay in his ward. It was the happiest and saddest time of my life, but moments I would cherish forever. Fearing the worst, I had to know. I needed to know. "Dad, why haven't we ever gone to your home? Why have we never met your family?"

He reached his large brown hand across the bed, combing my hair with his calloused fingers. His heavy breath sighing as he surrendered his inhibition to tell the truth.

"Mari, I left Chile under bad circumstances, and for a long time I wasn't allowed to return. I never wanted you to go through what happened to me and so I raised you to be Australian. I gave you an Australian education, taught you only English and never gave you the opportunity to meet your family or know your history. I believe because of this, I may have failed you. It's time for you to know the truth of why I left. Maybe then you will understand."

Breathe.

The day Pinochet took over will never escape my mind, he would say. A memory seared so deep into my conscious that it feels as if it just happened. At that time our family lived in the small coastal town of Copcecura; an insignificant place really, but one that meant the world to me.

When I wasn't teaching English at the local school, I would hitchhike to the next town over, named Buchupureo. Our town had no waves you see, and the ocean was full of Sea lions, which made the water smell. Buchupureo on the other hand was wonderful. Only a couple of houses; enough to call it a village and a café owned by an American surfer that wanted to *Vivir la vida* or something like that.

As you approached Buchupureo from the south, you summited a large hill that formed a separation point between the two towns. It was at this point, where I spent all my days. The strong, cold Humbolt current that carried icy water from Antarctica would hit the rocks and wrap around the point, forming great peeling waves; a fury when inside, but a beautiful spectacle of water slowly caressing its way across the black volcanic sand. Generally, the more hostile places were, the more beautiful, but this place was unique.

It was the 11th of September 1973. I was packing my lunch for what I hoped would be a fantastic day of surfing. The swell had been picking up over the past weeks, and this morning there was no wind. I was about to leave when I heard the phone ring. It was your grandmother. *"Hola... Hola! Hijito? Como estai, mi amor?"*

Whenever my mother, your grandmother would say this, I knew that she wanted something. It was always, "Can you help Mrs Doris to the bus station?" or, "I'm worried you are not eating enough, why don't you come around and I'll make you some Lentejas?" She was over-bearing at times, but that's how Chilean mothers were, and you had to love them for that.

But that day was different; she seemed worried. I didn't understand her concern. My mum wasn't one to take things too seriously, yet I could hear the worry in her voice.

"Son, I need you to go to Santiago and get your brother."

"Why, Mama?"

In a stammer that was hard for even Chileans to understand, she explained that there have been increasingly more protests in the streets against president Allende, and that she didn't feel safe for my brother anymore. She wanted him out of Santiago, at least until the protests were over. I tried to calm her down, reassuring her that my brother was fine, and agreeing to leave as soon as I got off the phone.

Having already packed my lunch for the surf trip, I jumped into my car and headed straight for Santiago. There were no main highways, and the trip would take all day. Typically, wasting a perfect day at the beach to drive to the city would upset me, but my brother, your uncle, lived in a nice house, with a spare bedroom, and his neighbour was very attractive.

As my dad got to this point in the story; he would shoot me a wink, as if he thought it was cool to talk about sexy old ladies in front of his daughter. Gross.

After seven hours of driving, I finally arrived at my brother's house. He lived in *'La Reina'*, a suburb of Santiago that housed wealthy people with fancy jobs. I knocked on the door and waited. Nobody answered. I knocked again, still nothing. Thinking he was out for a coffee, I used the spare key he had given me to let myself in and figured if I was going to have to wait for him, he could at least let me eat his food. Four hours and a full stomach later, he still had not come back. As I made my way to the spare bed, I wondered where he might be, before slipping into a dreamless sleep as I pulled the covers over my face.

I awoke to a furious banging on the front door, causing me to fall out of bed as my heart leaped into my mouth. Picking myself off the floor, I snuck to the front door. It was dark and I was reluctant to see who was there. It wasn't like Australia; you had to be cautious. The door banged a second time, catching me off guard and making me squeal like a little girl.

"Hermano, open up!"

Realising it was my brother; I opened the door, letting him into the house. He stared at me. I remember him just staring at me, as if I were an alien and he just couldn't believe I was real. I would never forget that moment, looking into his eyes and seeing pure fear, his soul reliving whatever it was he had just been through.

"We have to go," he urged. "I'll grab some things. Give me twenty minutes. I, I... I need twenty minutes."

Collapsing on the floor, my brother started to cry. I could feel my head throb, eyes dizzying as shock began to set in. Being the oldest, I wanted to make what was haunting him go away, to take his pain and replace it with happy thoughts of better times: Times perhaps at the beach when we were kids.

Through heaving breaths in an effort to compose himself, he recounted how the presidential palace had been bombed, killing President Allende. Augusto Pinochet, commander-in-chief of the military, had overthrown the government in a brutal takeover and established a military dictatorship. All supporters of the previous government were being rounded up and made to 'disappear'. Journalists and writers were being imprisoned and curfews established. It was hard to believe, and I was simultaneously filled with scepticism and fear, and questioned the validity of what he was describing. He looked at me with in disbelief.

"How could you not know? I saw them kill people, Hermano."

I don't know why, but for some reason this filled me with guilt, as if it were my responsibility to know what had taken place. His hands were shaking now, and I knew I had to distract him somehow.

"Come on. There is nothing we can do about it. We need to go. It is not safe here anymore. Go and pack your things, I'll bring the car around."

Nodding to acknowledge that he understood, my brother rose to his feet and staggered to his room, giving me time to fetch the car. Everything had changed since my arrival and I became acutely aware of the noise echoing up from the valley, drawing my attention to the ensuing chaos below.

Screaming, gunfire, car horns, the roar of a palace on fire, an orange blaze illuminated like a beacon of hope. A gross irony, as it defined something completely different. Like a deer in the headlights, I froze in fear, a million thoughts running through my head, none of which I could hold on to. I had to focus on my objective, getting the car.

Your uncle was already waiting by the door as I pulled the car up to the front of the house. He must have hastily shoved everything into his luggage without care, because he had four suitcases packed in a little over fifteen minutes. As curious as I was to know more, the look I had received earlier had made it clear that now was not the time to dick around. So without further hesitation, we quickly loaded the car and left immediately, travelling all night and switching drivers every so often so that the other could sleep or try to. We finally arrived at my house, exhausted from the long journey, but relieved to be distanced from the city. I made sure to call your grandmother to inform her we were back safely, before embracing my bed with open arms.

Being so distant from the capital, we believed that we were safer in Quirique than nearly anywhere else in Chile. For the following three months, we remained untouched from the effects of the coup de e'tat. This wouldn't last. We knew that we wouldn't be safe forever. Every morning and every night, we listened fervently to the radio, hoping for any news, crossing our fingers that it was good. It wasn't.

Walking home from the surf one Tuesday, I made sure to cut through the park, hoping to buy an ice cream for the remainder of the walk. Rounding the corner onto my street, I was surprised to find a military truck outside my house. What I saw next continues to haunt me today.

"Hermano! Hermano! Help!"

It was your uncle, being dragged from the house by four soldiers. A fifth soldier walked behind, carrying what appeared to be a jewellery box.

"What are these!" the officer screamed at my brother, saliva spraying from his mouth as he shoved a handful of papers from the box into his face. "Why do you have photos of the 'liberation'? Answer me!"

"Fuck you! That's evidence of war crimes. Your war crimes! Pig!"

The officer, outraged, lifted his foot, and smashed it into your uncle's face. I stood there watching, my body shaking in both fear and fury as I witnessed the scene unfold. I wanted to do something, anything, but knew any intervention would only escalate things to a point I was unwilling to go. Instead, I stood my ground and watched as your uncle's head flung back, blood pouring out of his nose. Valiantly, he tried standing, clearly ready to fight for his life.

"What are you going to do? Make me disappear? Do it, I dare you, but I swear, when I get out, I will hunt you down, and I will end you!"

Without further hesitation, the officer pulled out his pistol, and with the soldiers forcing your uncle onto his knees, shot him in the head.

"NOOOOOOOOO!!!" I screamed.

The blast from the gun must have deafened the soldiers momentarily, because they didn't turn their heads. I took a step towards them, ready to sprint and attack them with everything I had, and as I came around the corner and in plain view of the soldiers, I felt a sharp pain across the back of my head. My eyes began to water and I lost all strength in my legs. And that is all I can remember.

When I woke up, it was dark. I sat up slowly, my eyes beginning to adjust as I scanned my surroundings only to find myself in an unfamiliar place, a stranger's house perhaps. I felt confused, but before I could make another move, an older man, maybe in his sixties had rushed over and pushed me back down.

"Don't move; it's going to be all right."

"What happened? Where am I? Where is my brother?"

"Please, calm down. I will explain everything," the old man continued, trying to console me, but I was not listening.

"WHERE IS MY BROTHER? I NEED TO FIND MY BROTHER!"

"I'm sorry. I am so sorry. Your brother is dead."

The old man stared at me, tears rolling down his cheeks as he waited for my reaction. I was dumbstruck. Silent. I had witnessed your uncle being murdered. I knew this, yet hearing it just then had made it real. Suddenly I felt a loss such as I had never felt before. I remember not being able to breathe, rocking back and forth like a baby, unable to control my grief.

"*Esta bien hijo*," the old man repeated, consoling me as best he could. I didn't acknowledge him, instead closing my eyes, refusing to accept my newly discovered reality, and desperately trying to turn back time.

I stayed with the old man for another night, waiting for the police to leave town. I knew they would probably be looking for me as well, as it was my house and my brother who was caught with the photos. I was in no shape to be by myself anyway, and I think the old man knew that. He never left me out of sight, afraid of what I might do in anguish. I didn't do anything. I didn't even try; my emotional breakdown had ripped all physical strength and motivation to leave the safety of the bed. I could have shit myself and not even noticed. Eventually the soldiers did leave Quirique. They must have decided it wasn't worth staying in a 'boring' country town.

Finding strength again, I returned to my house to find it completely ransacked. In search of anything else, they had purposefully destroyed my belongings out of spite. My boards were broken, the furniture destroyed, and holes punched in the walls.

"You can stay at my house until we fix this," sympathised the old man, having accompanied me home.

There was no need. I couldn't go on living here. The army would still be looking for me. They probably believed I was an accomplice to my brother's 'treason'. Besides, all I could see was my brother's dead body, lying in the yard with a hole in his head and wondering why I didn't help him. My dear brother, Mario. That's right, Mari, you are named after your uncle, and you embody his spirit. I can see it in your eyes, in your character, in your soul. I'm certain he would be as proud of you as I am.

My dad paused at this moment and gave me a hug. It would seem a good a time as any, but I think it was more for him than for me. Then he would continue the story.

I stayed with the old man for another month, hiding in the house, and only going outside if it were absolutely necessary. I was afraid of the army finding and arresting me. Eventually however, I felt more and more restless, until one night, sitting together by the warm glow of the fire, it became too much.

"I can't continue on like this. I can't stay in this house forever."

"What are you going to do? You are associated with your brother, if they find you; I don't know that you will survive. I've heard the stories. They are cracking down on anyone who is a threat or publicly opposed to the government."

We sat in silence for a while, staring into the fireplace, and thinking of every possible scenario. I had grown fond of the old man. He had not only saved my life, but he had become a companion, my friend.

"I have an idea," he said suddenly, looking up at me. "But it is going to be risky."

"Do I have any other choice?" I scoffed. "I can't stay here for the rest of my life. What did you have in mind?"

By the dim light of the flickering fire, he informed me of his family's sailboat, unused, well stocked, and close by, about three hours up the coast. Like a secret, he explained that I could take it and sail west. It was a long shot, and I may perish along the way, but there were a lot of countries taking political refugees, and it would be worth trying. I couldn't cross the border to Argentina, they would just send me straight back to the Chilean Government, so this was my only option if I wanted to have a life.

"What do you think?"

I sat there for a long time. I remember getting up and making a cup of tea. I needed time to think. The old man wasn't proposing a cruisy day trip to the beach. He was suggesting that I should sail across the entire Pacific Ocean.

"But I don't know how to sail."

He laughed out loud. "No, not at all. It's a bit of a catch twenty-two. I can teach you the theory tonight and then you can leave tomorrow. Consider it an adventure."

After another period of silence and with limited options, I finally made up my mind.

"Okay, I'll do it."

There was so much to organise from that point. I had to pack anything I could take with me, obtain all of my documentation that I still had left after the raid to use as identification when I landed wherever it was I was going. I had to write a letter to my mum and let her know what was happening, and I had to learn how to sail. It was going to be a long night.

I spent the rest of the evening at the table, listening intently, writing down everything I could, and drawing diagrams, instructions, and weather patterns. Everything. By 3am, I was shattered. I went to bed and fell asleep immediately, only to be woken up at 7am.

"Hey, get up," the old man whispered, shaking my shoulder gently. "I have just called my cousin and he will have the boat ready in a few hours. We have to leave in 30 minutes."

I grumbled through a drool-laden pillow, acknowledging that I had understood. I felt like I had been hit by a truck. Getting up, I could see that the old man had left coffee for me on the table. I got up, grabbed the coffee and sat down at the table. Using the available pen and piece of paper still there from the night before, I started to write to my mother, your grandma, explaining everything and hoping that she could hold onto me, even though I was leaving without saying goodbye.

Finishing the letter, I snuck outside and discreetly placed the letter in her mailbox, before making my way over to my house, praying that no soldiers were around. When I arrived, I immediately grabbed the backpack that I had used for travelling through Patagonia the year before and shoved everything I possibly could inside: Clothes, jewellery, passports, important documents, money, and photos.

Overjoyed to discover that of all my boards the soldiers broke, my three favourites were still intact: A white short board, 10-foot-long board, and brand new minimal. I hastily packed the last few items, before making my way to the door, only to notice something out of the corner of my eye glint in the early morning sun that streamed in through the front window. Leaning forward to pick up the object from the floor, I realised it was a photo of your uncle and I from our surf trip to Argentina four years ago.

There we were arms around each other's shoulders, surfboards by our sides, and grins larger than life. We had just come out of the surf when that photo was taken, all day cruising down two footers that peeled for what seemed like forever, only to finish the day off by chasing girls at the local pub.

I stared at the photo for a long time, taking deep breaths as my hands trembled, the photo shaking into a blur as a tear rolled down the bridge of my nose, dripped into the air, landing on the photo.

"I'm sorry, Hermano."

With that, I let the photo fall to the ground as I strode out the door. The memory too recent and overpowering to take with me, as if to say, 'I couldn't save you then, why should I carry you with me now.'

"Are you ready?"

I followed the old man to his truck and we proceeded to load my bag and tie down the boards. Before I knew it, we were ready to go.

"Is there anything else you need before we leave?" he questioned.

"No, let's drive."

The next three hours passed in silence. Placing my head against the window, I steadily drifted in and out of sleep, only to be kept awake by the constant reel of worries traveling on repeat through my mind. I didn't know if I would ever return, and certainly had not foreseen I would not see your grandma again. I had left the country many times before, but never like this, and certainly not without knowing what to expect.

We finally reached the boat around 11am. Being a Sunday, everybody was at home, leaving the docks deserted, and a silence filling the air. With no one around, and the Chilean Navy busy in the north reorganising themselves under the new leadership and ridding themselves of disloyal sailors, it seemed I would be able to sail away from the Chilean coast without complications, notwithstanding my sinking it.

I loaded my bag and boards onto the boat, making sure I had all the necessary documentation. After one last run through of the basic sailing skills with the old man, and double-checking that there was enough food on board to last the next three months, it was then time to cast off. I looked at the old man, hoping to convey the gratitude that I could never express in words, and hiding the pain of saying goodbye to another that I have come to love.

"You saved my life. How will I ever repay you?"

"Live to save another life, one day." Breathe.

Chapter 2

"Shit!"

I awoke to the heat of the rising sun cracking my lips, reminding me of another big night of inebriation. Sitting up slowly, I wiped the sand from my brow, and facing an empty beach, I wondered what on earth happened last night. Reaching for the half-smoked joint from my back pocket, I tried to understand how I ended up here. A light offshore breeze played with my long brown hair.

I walked slowly back to my car, bewildered by the fact that it was a summer morning at Alexandra Headland and no one was at the beach. No one trying to escape the heat, get a surf in before work or even trying to get in shape as they resolved on New Year's Eve, only to give up 15 minutes later and grab a coffee at the surf club.

Rusted out from all the ocean spray, the only good things about my old car were the roof racks that held my surfboards. She wasn't exactly a kombi, but she was mine and she was loyal. Reaching up to unstrap my mini mal, I convinced myself that everyone else was enjoying a Sunday morning sleep in. Lucky me, waves to myself!

I just couldn't resist. It was too perfect to go home and sleep off last night's bender; instead, I made my way down to the beach. Seeing someone approaching from the far side of the beach, I squinted to see if I knew him, but he was too far away to recognise, seemingly a blur, as if he might not be there at all. Deciding it didn't really matter, and with too much stoke to care, I paddled out into what I hoped would be a great session, the light offshore breeze just enough to clean up the southeast swell that broke off the bluff on the south side of 'Alex' beach.

I paddled around the outside of the break and was instantly transformed, overcome by emotion, giving me a feeling of absolute presence. An inundation of positive thoughts drove me to make the most of a spectacular day. Here we go, Mari, focus. Paddle! Paddle! Paddle! Rights all day baby! And this was it. This was everything. This was why I was here. This was what I lived for. Two hours passed, then three, the whole time in my own company. I took wave after wave, their size not diminishing with the losing tide. It was a surreal experience that could cure anything, even my hangover.

Duck diving to cool off, I re-emerged on the surface to find a wall of water racing towards me. Turning hard, I paddled with all the strength I had left to catch the largest wave of the day. I took off deep and was already caught inside the tube before I was able to get a good footing. I leaned forward to gain speed and avoid getting swallowed by Poseidon's blowhole. As I emerged from the tube I pushed hard on the back of the board, slowing down and allowing myself to get back in the pocket.

"This is magic," I shouted, turning off the top of the wave, completely captivated by the ocean. "I can't believe this is rea…"

Smack! Two tonnes of water right in the face. The wave closing out had taken me by surprise, throwing me backwards off my board, forcing me to cover my head to avoid the rocks which appeared with the bluff's low tide. It wasn't exactly the way I wanted to end the great session, but being a little disoriented, I decided to call it quits.

I made my way back to shore and couldn't help but think of how lucky I was to live here. The Sunshine Coast, a region of South East Queensland, made up of a network of coastal towns that connected Caloundra on the southern end to Noosa in the north. It was a very diverse place, with each town having its own character, albeit sharing a common culture of slow-paced, easy-going attitudes with a respect for the ocean and the lifestyle it provided.

Having been born here, my early years were spent never more than ten minutes from a beach. I couldn't remember ever being out of the water. Swimming lessons, then nippers, lifesaving, surfing, a lifetime of salty hair and sandy clothes. It was easy to know who the locals were, even if only by their faces, and likewise, they recognised you. "Hey, mate, how's it goin'?" I greeted Boedi, finally reaching my car.

"Yeah, good, Mari, Sick waves yeah? I'm spewin' I missed it. How'd ya go?"

Boedi, my oldest friend, having met in Nippers Surf Lifesaving School when we were six, shared a common love for surfing. Originally from Torquay, Victoria, he had a great capacity for knowing where the best waves were. Down to earth, kind, witty, he could always be relied on to give you a ride, which I took advantage of a little too often. Sorry mate.

"Brilliant! Absolutely sick session. The stoke is high."

"I saw you get smashed on that last one. You're losing your touch, mate."

I shoved Boedi aside cheekily as I strapped my board onto the car and questioned why he wasn't out there with me, soaking in the rays and ripping on the waves. It wasn't like Boedi to miss a surf sesh, he checked the report every day and even missed work for the best conditions. Mumbling that he had something important to do, I knew he is lying. He never lied to me, and I wanted to know why. So I pushed for an answer, knowing I must have sounded like a little girl asking why on repeat.

"Well," he paused, "I may have stayed at someone's house last night."

It was hard to hide my jealousy as Boedi revealed how he met a girl from Brisbane, his voice even lower now, as if he didn't want to tell me any more than he had to. It wasn't that I was into him, he has just always been around, and as far as I could recall, he had never stayed at a girl's house. I tightened the last strap down on my board, securing it to the car, before turning suddenly to face Boedi. "She better not stop you from surfing with me. Some city bitches are nuts."

"Mate, calm down. No one will ever stop me from surfing."

"Good."

I hopped into the car and immediately made the mistake of putting on my seat belt too fast, burning the side of my hip with the seatbelt lock, branding my ignorance as I drove off. Rule number one: Australian summers turned seatbelts into hot irons! The pain subsided after a couple of choice words, and I lowered the driver's side window in an effort to escape the hot box from hell.

The drive to my house was pathetic; 15 minutes from the beach, but it was the only area I could afford to rent. It wasn't necessarily a bad area. Okay, it was shit, and was really far from the beach. What did you want me to say? That socioeconomically speaking, the area in comparison to other areas in Australia was...blah blah.

Luckily, I could crash at Boedi's on the weekends, well hopefully I still could.

I pulled into the driveway to see a yellow scooter parked against the garage, indicating that my flatmate Sandy was home. She was an interesting character; with short black hair, pale skin, a nose ring, and a quiet reserved voice, behaving and speaking like a proper lady, as the nuns had forced to her since her first day at catholic school. We were as different as chalk and cheese, but she was nice and we got on well. I started undoing the straps on the board when I heard the familiar screech of the front screen door opening and blurted out a casual hello without bothering to turn around.

"Hello, how are you doing today?"

"Yeah mate, good thanks."

I knew I should probably be more conscious of how I spoke, but this was the way I have always spoken, loud and proud, educated in thought, but not conformed by speech. Sometimes I'd like to sound more like Sandy, but the shoe just didn't fit. "Weird day though, woke up on the beach with a hangover. I don't remember drinking, must've drowned myself last night."

"Oh… Okay, I understand. I'll just return this beer to the fridge then."

Not wanting to offend her, I politely put my hand out to receive the beverage. Sandy went back inside and after a refreshing first sip, I took my boards off the car, storing them in the garage before heading into the house. I was feeling on top of the world, yet I had nothing to do for the rest of the day.

"Hey, Sandy, what are ya up to? Keen for a Sunday sesh? Boeds is probably gonna stop by later."

Sandy, the poor girl, had always had a massive crush on Boedi and I felt bad for manipulating her, but I didn't want to drink alone. Besides, she needed to get out more. By get out, I meant to the back porch with more beers.

"Oh, Boedi is coming over? I suppose I had better not be rude. Okay, I could have a drink."

"That's my girl," I responded gleefully, patting her on the back and handing her a champagne glass filled with her favourite bubbles.

Taking a seat across the table, I proceeded to recount the entire morning: From waking up all alone on a deserted beach, to the strange character in the distance, not knowing who he was, but gaining a weird sense of familiarity. This stuff fascinated Sandy. She loved the mysterious and unexplainable and would sometimes stay up all night with me, drinking and discussing an array of topics from the possibility of alien life to government cover-ups.

"I don't understand," interrupted Sandy. "What's so strange about the guy on the beach?"

"I dunno, but when I saw him my heart began to race and a sense of intense *deja vu* came over me, but I couldn't place it. Who was he?"

"That's not strange. You pretty much live at the beach. You would know everyone there, even if just by their face."

We sat there in silence for some time, slowly sipping our drinks. With not much else to say, Sandy pulled out her phone, and from the movement of her thumb, I could guess confidently that she was mindlessly scrolling through Facebook. I continued to sit there deep in thought, reliving the morning, and curious to know who Boedi's new girl was. Speak of the devil.

"Hey guys!" Boedi announced his presence as he slipped through the back door.

"Hey, mate! I thought you might stop by. Beer?"

"Yeah sure, how are you, Sandy?"

Sandy had forgotten about Boedi and jumped, spilling her drink, before squeaking a friendly hello back. Her cheeks reddened as she attempted to make herself invisible by sinking further into her chair. The rest of the afternoon passed in an array of conversation, mostly around surfing, the forecast, parties and life. Occasionally, Sandy popped in a word or two, only to regress back to the safety of social media. Before we knew it, darkness had surrounded us and the lights flicked on.

"Shit, I didn't realise the time, I gotta go," Boedi said, standing up and grabbing his jacket and keys in haste.

I shot him a wink and cracked a joke about having to run off to his needy city girl. He refused to acknowledge my remark, leaving in silence but careful to grab a beer on his way out. Sandy and I continued to enjoy each other's company, evening soon turned into night as we sat in silence, listening to the radio as I emptied the fridge of the remaining bottles.

My stomach bulged, bloated from all the beer, making it uncomfortable to stand as I attempted to answer nature's call. With Sandy already in hysterics, I tried to compose myself, but fell into the kitchen, tripping on the step as I made my way through the door. I continued to struggle in a hopeless attempt to navigate the ever-turning doorways and spinning halls. Through some miracle, I found the toilet, finally relieving myself just in time, my stomach shrinking as I disposed of the 12 beers I had consumed throughout the night. The effect of the alcohol was taking its toll, and deciding it was too difficult to put on my pants, abandoned them on the toilet floor as I left in search of my room. Finding it after considerable effort, I fell onto the bed and stared at the ceiling. The room was spinning and I felt as if I would fly off the mattress at any moment.

Unable to fall asleep, I just lied there, not trusting myself to leave the safety of my bed until I was sober. My mind began to drift from place to place, and before I knew it, I was back to the first time I learnt how to surf.

It was clear day, the sun already halfway up the sky, illuminating Tea Tree Bay in a brilliance of aqua blues and surrounded by a jungle of evergreen trees, waving in the light offshore breeze which made its way over the ridge.

I laid on my dad's board facing the shore. I had been out in the surf for a while now and was ready to take on my biggest challenge yet: Standing up and riding a wave. This was my shot. After practising all morning, this would be my first attempt to ride a wave on my own.

I couldn't see what was coming but my dad reassured me with kind words and guaranteed I would surf a great big wave. He was standing next to me holding the board to maintain my balance until just the right moment to let go. I felt safe in his shadow and having him guide me gave me the confidence I needed.

"Are you ready?" he asked, keeping an eye on the one-foot waves as they approached.

Overcome with the emotion and determination of a five-year-old excited to catch her first wave, I immediately started paddling with all my strength. My dad was still holding onto the board and I was going nowhere. All of a sudden, I felt the water begin to rise from under me and heard my dad yell, "Go!" I paddled harder than ever, and thanks to an encouraging push, I launched forward, cruising down the wave at record speed.

I pushed as hard as I could from the board just as I had been shown. Lifting my left knee, I tried to step as high as I could in order to find the perfect footing to stand up. Exhilaration was growing inside of me, and I believed it was actually going to happen.

Releasing a scream of joy, I let go of the board and tried to stand up. The board instantly wobbled underneath me, causing me to fall backwards, splashing into the water, the sky slowly disappearing under a cloud of water.

"I was so close!"

Re-emerging on the surface of the water, I jumped on my board and started paddling back towards my father. He was standing there, water at waist height, staring at me and smiling from ear to ear. As I drew closer to him I saw the next set coming towards me, the waves barely big enough to move my board, yet massive to me, with no idea how to get past them and back to my dad.

"What do I do?"

"Paddle hard, Mari! You have to paddle hard. When the wave gets to you, hold onto your board and let the wave go under you."

So supportive was my father, finding comical cuteness in my 'dire situation'. What seemed like minutes was only seconds, what appeared very far away was actually quite close. The perception of the world through the eyes of a child was nothing less than awe inspiring, everything new and greater than oneself.

The wave drew closer as I grasped the rails of my board just as my father had instructed, staring ahead with utter determination, and bracing for impact as the wave arrived. Then it was over. Stunned at the lack of drama, happiness flooded back, replacing fear as I completed the long paddle back to my father's side.

"I don't know why I fell. I did everything you told me to."

"You need to look at the shore," Dad instructed. "When you stand up, you need to look where you want to go. Your body follows your eyes. If you look at the beach, you will catch the wave. If you look at your feet, you will fall over. Understand?"

I nodded in acknowledgement, focused on my newfound key to success as I set back into position for the next wave.

"Here we go, Mari! You've got this one."

The next wave approached and I paddled with everything I had, gaining momentum without the assistance of a friendly push. I was all on my own and understood that I would be prouder if I succeeded through my own merit. The wave finally arrived, pushing me forward, and careful to stare straight ahead, I stood up, the board wobbling under my feet. I extended my arms to regain my balance and continued to focus on the trees lining the shore. Before I knew it, I was surfing.

"YAAAY! I did it! I caught my first wave! Daddy, did you see?"

"I'm so proud of you, Mari. I love you." Breathe.

Chapter 3

The light burned the insides of my eyelids as I rolled over, trying to escape yet another hangover. I lied there groaning for another hour before finally giving in and pulling the blankets down from my face. "Err, I need to stop drinking."

Making my way to the kitchen, I realised the full extent of my bender: Handprints on the wall, a knocked-over plant, and as it turns out, I missed the toilet, gross. The mess was cleaned up quickly and I crossed my fingers that Sandy had gone to bed without noticing, before making my way to the kitchen where I hoped to find bacon in the fridge. To my delight I found Sandy instead, cooking what looked to be a feast fit for a king. I noticed her obvious amusement at my sickly state as I mumbled a good morning and sat on the stool facing her. The clock struck 11:00am, and I realised I had slept away half the day.

Being the sweet girl that she was, Sandy had prepared for my struggle and kindly served me two eggs on toast. From the second the food hit the plate; all manners went out the window, making the eggs disappear similar to a vacuum sucking up dirt off the floor. The food worked its magic and I felt better as I help myself to a second serving, being sure to take a couple of headache tablets with my last bite of buttered toast. "Sorry about last night. I didn't realise I was that drunk."

"Not a problem," Sandy replied, a smile growing on her face. "It was pretty funny. At one point, you were pretending to surf, making all sorts of action noises before declaring yourself the best surfer in the world. You put on quite a performance."

Slightly embarrassed, I couldn't remember last night at all, but Sandy continued to reassure me that it wasn't as bad as I thought, that I gave myself motion sickness and ended up stumbling off to the toilet and out of sight.

"Don't you have to leave for work soon?" asked Sandy, suddenly realising the time.

"Oh shit. I have to go!"

Work dragged by in monotony, serving customers and selling surfboards. Of course, I always had a sneaky beer at the surf club after work to liven things up, but like everyone else on the coast or I suppose even in the world, I quickly fell into the routine of working for the weekend and not appreciating what I had on a daily basis.

Saturday finally arrived and I was already on my way to the beach before the sun had fully risen. The surf was sitting at a comfortable three to four feet in height with strong east winds, indicating that the waves would be dumping and the water would resemble a washing machine. Saltwater splashed into my face as I paddled through the surf, navigating the white wash and finding an open area at the back of the waves. From here I could see the entire shoreline, allowing me to watch for breaks to open up as other surfers left in annoyance with the poor conditions, giving me more room amongst the waves rather than trying to fight for a prime position.

Jumping off my board, I dove underwater, floating just below the surface with my eyes closed; the gentle surge of the sea rocking me back and forth like a cradle. After a few moments of utter relaxation, I opened my eyes and was perplexed to find myself surrounded by a reef. All by myself in a blue world, I was accompanied only by silent movement of the multi coloured coral which extended beyond the underwater horizon. The silence was broken by a soft rumble like thunder from an oncoming storm. I looked up to discover the source of the noise; waves crashing down on the surface, creating magnificent bursts of white water. What fury. What beauty. Raw, destructive energy leaving me untouched in order to watch the spectacle as it unfolded. It felt like a dream, yet very much alive.

Of course, it couldn't be real. I was not in the same place that I dove into only moments before. So, where was I? My body rose towards the surface, growing closer and closer to the bashing waves. Suddenly very aware of the danger I was in, I started to panic, squeezing me eyes shut and preparing for the worst.

Nothing happened. Peeking through squinted eyes, I no longer saw the coral and the smashing waves were gone. The brief experience had left me slightly shaken and struggling to comprehend what just happened, I broke the surface to take a deep, much-needed breath. Looking for anything familiar in an effort to get my bearings and calm myself down I surveyed my surroundings. Nothing had changed and I was disappointed to see that the surf was now more packed than ever. There was a gap between a group of guys sitting in the perfect position to catch the lip of the wave and as I took my place between them it was evident that everyone now was bothered by the crowd, the vibe echoing throughout the bay, stating that today was not a good day for me to be a smartass.

Noticing the incoming set, everyone turned in unison and charged the wave. With the lip coming straight for me and knowing that I was clear to take the drop, I stood up, leaning forward hard on my front foot to gain as much speed as possible. Out of the corner of my eye, I could see a surfboard coming towards me and immediately stomped hard on the back of the board, desperately trying to brake whilst turning towards the shore in order to avoid a collision as the board rider roared down the wave.

For a split second, I thought that this arsehole would pass by me, when all of a sudden, my board came to a halt, the crunch of breaking fibreglass noticeably loud as fins cut their way into the side of my board. I launched forward, diving headfirst towards the bottom of the wave. Out of pure reflex, I covered the top of my head and hoped to God that I didn't hit the sand bank below.

Emerging from the water untouched, fury grew inside of me as I turned to see the culprit attempting to get back on his board in an effort to flee. Clearly, he had no experience or any idea of surfing etiquette. If anyone was going to give him a lesson, it was going to be me, right now, and he wasn't going to like it. "What the fuck mate? You need to look to make sure others aren't on the wave. You could have really hurt someone. You ran right into me, dickhead."

"Sorry," he apologised half-heartedly. "I thought I had it. It was a great wave. There's no need to be a bitch."

Unable to contain myself, I punched him right in the face, causing him to yell an array of swearwords through a muffled hand as he tried to contain the blood now flowing from what I expected to be a broken nose. Too infuriated to say anything else, I turned and paddled back towards the shore, reaching the beach and immediately inspecting the damage. My board was ruined and I had no choice but to end the day, incredibly upset with no idea how I was going to be able to pay for a board repair. With the broken board now strapped onto the car, I returned to the surf club desperately in need of a drink and couldn't think of a more convenient place than the bar upstairs. Steve was working behind the bar and greeted me with a smirk. "Back so soon? This is your third time this week."

"Yeah, well, this one is well deserved. Someone just smashed into me and broke my board."

"Really? Well then this one is my treat."

"Cheers, mate. In that case I'll take two."

I shot him a wink to indicate that I was joking, but without hesitation he immediately filled a second pint, sliding it in front of me before whispering, 'Don't tell anyone.' The first one slipped down like a child on a water slide. The second one I sipped more slowly, my nerves now relaxed as I continued to chat with Steve, who had nothing better to do in an empty bar. Dehydrated from the surf, I could feel the alcoholic effect of the beers faster than usual. Starting my third pint, this one I insisted on paying for. The more I drank, the more attractive Steve became, until alcohol and hormonal attraction collided, giving me the urge to kiss him, to feel him all over, right now.

Leaning across the bar, I waved my finger in an effort to draw Steve in as if to tell him a secret and through slurred words invited him to drink with me. On the count of three we shot back a slightly tinted liquid of Steve's choice, burning my throat in satisfaction as I slammed the glass back down on the bar. Steve said something, but I wasn't listening, because there was a drop of whiskey hanging from the edge of his moustache, and I wanted to lick it off. "Hey, Steve," I slurred, quickly becoming increasingly incomprehensible. "I'm a little drunk. Can you drive me home, you know, for safety?"

"No worries."

Driving home, the view of passing buildings faded away as I leaned over and started playing with his hair, making nonsensical comments to myself as the radio played the latest hit by some artist with funky hair. My head found his shoulder as my hand snuck onto his leg, moving back and forth to massage his thigh. This relaxed me more than Steve and my mind drifted as my eyelids closed, only to be jolted awake as we pulled into my driveway. Without hesitation I suggested that Steve come in for more beers. He followed me inside. It was his first time over and I hoped my room wasn't a mess. Now that I think about it, it was the first time we had ever spent time together outside of the pub. He had no idea what was about to happen.

Unexpectedly, I grabbed him, holding firmly around his waist with no intention of letting go. For a second we stared at each other, as if consenting to what would follow, before pushing him backwards into my room and onto my bed, sitting on top of him so he knew that I wanted it. Lost in my own world, I began to dry hump his crotch, simultaneously ripping my shirt open in one smooth motion. His shirt came off as I worked my way up his chest with my lips, slowly heading in the direction of his mouth as my hands slid south toward his crotch.

Just like that, it was on. Pants coming off in unison before flipping over again. Steve took charge as I bit the pillow in ecstasy. He continued to thrust as I squeezed the headboard in delight, unable to contain the orgasms flowing through the sheets. Holy shit, Steve could fuck. I didn't know how long it lasted, but it felt like time had stopped completely. However, with one final groan, Steve was done, rolling over and lying onto his back, sweat was pouring onto the sheets as a cheeky smirk made its way across his face.

I made my way to the bathroom to clean myself up and took a moment to wash my face. Completely sober now, a feeling of loneliness came over me and the urge to return to the comfort of a random bartender sleeping in my bed became overwhelming.

Breathe…

A burning ray of light streamed through the window. Sweat poured from me in the intense heat of a shared bed as I awoke to a feeling of extreme thirst. The air burned my parched throat as I pulled apart chapped lips in an effort to breathe and sitting up, I momentarily forgot that Steve was beside me. Slipping out of bed, I grabbed a shirt and pants from the cupboard and made my way to the bus stop to go and collect my car. It was already thirty degrees Celsius and I wondered if it was going to storm.

Arriving at the surf club, I was surprised by the larger than normal number of people lined up to buy a coffee. It took twenty minutes to finally receive my usual flat white and in an effort to avoid the unbearable commotion of the surf club café, I headed for the quieter section of the beach. I walked north along the stretch which connects Alex and Maroochydore beaches. Close to a kilometre in length, it had fewer people, with a small number of locals, power walkers, and surfers waiting for the break between the sets before entering the ocean. The walk was aimless, allowing me to enjoy this exact moment of peace, undistracted by the outside world or my internal one, the sun's heat complementing the coffee perfectly to wake me up.

Halfway through my coffee, I noticed a father and his daughter throwing a ball into the surf for their dog to chase and sat down in the sand to watch. The dad was laughing and the daughter, maybe five years old, was in complete bliss as she entertained the dog, giving him a wet and sandy hug every time he returned with the ball. I smiled at the scene in front of me. The sun reappeared from behind a cloud, perfectly illuminating the father daughter moment that would be remembered for a lifetime: Dad threw the ball, the dog chased it and the daughter chased the dog, paying no attention as the last of the white water bounced off of their legs on its way in to shore.

The little girl screamed and giggled as she jumped up and down, thoroughly soaking her dress as she called for the dog to return the ball. Like a shadow, her dad snuck up from behind and in one swift movement, yelled 'BOO!' whilst lifting the unsuspecting girl off her feet and placing her over his shoulder. He spun her around again and again, her voice omitting another gleeful scream as she was taken for the ride of her life.

Watching the obvious and genuine joy emitted by their presence, their connection made me smile, and for a moment it reminded me of the joy I had felt as a little girl; ignorant of life, yet completely filled with a desire to discover each new day. It was as if I was watching a family video. So similar to my childhood memories, I was confused by the sudden sense of *deja vu* and needed to remind myself this wasn't a dream or a memory. It was a real situation that somehow stirred an emotional response based on a shared experience.

The last drops of coffee made their way out of the cup and into my mouth. I savoured the flavour of the now lukewarm liquid as it disappeared, providing one last jolt of energy before standing up and starting my walk back to the Alex Surf Club. The sun disappeared behind another cloud as I took one final look over my shoulder to see the little girl running towards her dad, before turning back, ending my walk down memory lane.

"Shit, my board!"

I ran to my car, having forgotten all about yesterday's surfing accident. A part of me didn't want to believe that my board was ruined. My heart sunk as I opened the boot to find the same two gashes glaring back at me, but on inspecting the damage closer, it seemed the cuts to my board were repairable. The first was deep into the side, but not so deep that it would easily break under pressure. The second, right across the top but hardly scratching the epoxy. With the proper repair work, my board could be restored almost as good as new without any loss of integrity to its strength.

Fortunately, my boss shaped boards in the back room of the surf shop where I worked and hoping to get lucky, I took my board inside and smiled at my good fortune as I heard the sound of a sander coming from the back room. Screaming over the noise, I explained the situation, lifting my board for him to see and stating that I didn't have the money to fix it. He gritted his teeth, an indication that the damage was a lot worse than I thought it would be. Without even a word, my heart dropped, and I feared the worst. "Can you fix it?"

"I can fix anything. But it won't be easy. I'll show you how to fix it, but you have to do the actual work. I'll be here to guide you, that way you'll learn."

"Absolutely, I can do that!"

"Oh, and one more thing. You owe me a six-pack beer."

Every night for the following week, I stayed after work to help fix my board. The six pack turned into a case, which we shared equally as I sanded down the damaged area, applied an epoxy fiberglass mix and filled the cuts, only to let it set overnight and repeat the process again, until the fourth night, when the final sanding was complete and last touch ups applied. The board looked as good as new and I was impressed with my work, especially considering how much we drank while repairing it.

The next few weeks went by in a flash. When the surf was good, I surfed, and when it wasn't, I worked. Soon enough, the days started blurring together, until before I knew it, it was my birthday. The twelfth of June, my favourite day of the year. I didn't really think of myself as special, but it was a great excuse to do anything I wanted without considering other people. This sounded bad, but it gave me a feeling of freedom. The last few years, I would go on a surf trip by myself, just packing up and going, rarely telling anyone where or for how long. This year was different. I was twenty-six, and for the first time, I didn't want to be alone on my birthday.

The sound of the ceiling fan woke me from a dreamless sleep and rolling over to grab my phone, I whispered 'Happy birthday' to myself. My melancholy was made worse upon reading the surf report and realising that I would have more luck catching waves in a bathtub; the lack of storms and offshore winds had turned the ocean into a lake, forcing me to change my plans from the only thing I could imagine doing on such a special day. I had forgotten to tell anyone that I wasn't going away, and sat up to the realisation that I didn't have any plans at all.

My phone buzzed, causing me to drop it in surprise, it falling and smacking me in the mouth. The instant throbbing felt as my lip grew in size, a tear forming in my eye as I tried acting like nothing happened. I answered with a 'Herro', ignoring the now dissipating pain in my bottom lip.

"HAPPY BIRTHDAY!" greeted a familiar voice. "What are you doin', ya slob?"

"I'm just waking up, Boeds, stop yelling. What's up?"

"I was thinking of going spearfishing and free diving off Double Island Point. Do you want to come?"

"Yeah I do! That sounds awesome!" I yelled with excitement, playing with my hair in the mirror as I tried to pull myself together. "When are we leaving?"

"Right now," says Boedi. "I'm outside."

Ocean on my right, coastal forest on my left, and in front of me, sixty kilometres of pristine sandy beach. The Noosa North Shore drive was the best way to access Double Island Point and with Boedi's four-wheel drive we easily cruised over the sand, relishing the sensation of being in the middle of nowhere whilst recklessly sitting on the windowsill to take in the wind.

Our arrival was marked by a lighthouse-crested bluff. I watched how the ocean moved as I helped Boedi unload the paddleboards; the conditions hadn't changed since earlier and the light westerly offshore wind was a good sign for a day of free diving. The small swell an indication of perfect conditions.

Our objective for the day was Wolf Rock: A random section of reef rising out of the sea which a colony of grey nurse sharks called home for their winter breeding season. A spectacle to watch, but still early in the season, we were hoping to get lucky.

We paddled for maybe an hour, the bluff slowly shrinking behind us as we headed out to sea. Being out of the tourist season, I was happy to see that no other boats or divers were about; we had the whole place to ourselves!

At the first buoy we tied in our paddleboards. No need for an anchor, these would ensure that we had a place to rest and that our boards didn't float away. Too excited to waste any more time, I shoved my goggles on and plunged into the water, inspecting the surrounding reef. Slightly murky, with only ten metres of visibility, I could just make out the sharks swimming below. It was an impressive demonstration of nature, but observing through the roof of their world was not enough to satisfy my urge. To see the world as they do. To be amongst them. "This is going to be great!"

"Do you know what to do?" Boedi asked as he checked the lines to make sure the boards were secure.

"What do you mean? I just hold my breath and dive down and look at stuff. It doesn't seem that hard."

"Not quite. Come over here and I'll show you."

I swam to Boedi, who showed me how to float on my back, placing his hands under me to provide extra support. Instructing me like a swim coach, he told me to breathe in for five seconds and then exhale for twenty. We continued this for five minutes, until I was so relaxed I was certain I no longer needed water to float.

"Great work mate! Now on the count of three, I want you to roll over and dive down. Be careful to move slowly with your hands by your side. Try to stay as relaxed as possible. Ready? One, two, three, go!"

I turned and dived, taking one big sweep with my arms and placing them at my side to gain momentum as instructed. I kicked slowly, using my fins to propel me the rest of the way down. At five metres, I released the pressure built up in my ears by blowing through a plugged nose. At ten metres I could see the bottom. At fifteen metres, I stopped in awe, maintaining my buoyancy in a seated position, floating as if supported by an imaginary chair. What appeared in front of me left me awestruck. The rock appeared to be moving as hundreds of grey nurse sharks swam in circles, chasing each other around the reef, looking to impress a mate.

I remained motionless, rooted to one place as I watched the sharks swim past in a blur. Hypnotised by their movements, I allowed everything else to fall away, providing me with an immense clarity and sense of absolute presence in their world.

"Ow!"

Jolted from my daze in fright, I spun around to find Boedi tapping me on the shoulder. My heart was racing and I felt the desperate urge to breathe as oxygen was pumped from my blood in fear. My diaphragm convulsed in an attempt to force my mouth open, my body reacting to the intense pressure it was going through. Boedi gave me a thumbs up indicating that I needed to resurface, so I grabbed him under the arm and began to rise, leaving the underwater fantasy behind, watching it slowly sink into darkness.

"And breathe! In two seconds, out five, in two seconds, out five," coached Boedi as we breached the surface. He moved his hand up and down as he counted, conducting me as I took in mouthfuls of air. Slowly, my breath returned to normal, the pressure fading as the safety of fresh air flooded back through my body.

"You were underwater for four minutes," exclaimed Boedi. "That's the longest I've ever seen anyone hold their breath."

"Not bad considering I don't train. Could you imagine if I did this for a living?"

"Maybe you could, but you'd probably have to stop drinking so much. Haha!"

I splashed him, initiating an all-out wrestling match. It didn't take long for Boedi to win, shoving my head under water and declaring himself king of the sea. We regained our composure and continue diving down on Wolf Rock, taking turns to mind the boards, as the other explored the far reaches of the ocean below.

Time and time again I dived. With the shock and awe of the first experience past, pure joy kicked in as I joined the sharks in their dance, swimming around the reef in their company with the occasional pat along their back and fins. The sharks were so docile that at no point in time did I feel threatened. Most assumptions about sharks were false. First of all, sharks were just one of many marine species, and like any species, they came in all shapes and sizes. Some were small and eat sea grass, some aggressive and eat big fish. In the end, they are a part of the oceanic ecosystem, acting on instinct to survive, and nearly all attacks on humans were a case of mistaken identity or a defensive measure when they felt threatened. If you could respect their environment and presence, you could swim with them as comfortably as I did now.

I followed a large shark as he split off from the group, swimming slightly out from the rock. Something had caught its eye. It slowed to a glide, stream lining its body to maintain forward momentum without disturbing the water around it, essentially hiding itself in plain sight.

A small stingray appeared, flying along in ignorance of its future demise as it came into clear view of the shark. In a flash the shark reacted, whipping itself forward with tremendous speed. Within half a second it reached the stingray, biting into it without hesitation. The stingray violently flailed, but with the shark's strong grip, biting directly over the body, the ray had no chance. As blood seeped through the shark's teeth, it claimed its prize, victorious in its hunt and well fed for the rest of the day.

Although not afraid, blood plus sharks equal a situation I did not want to be around. I headed to the surface, leaving the scene as fast as I could. My suspicions were confirmed as six more sharks rushed to the blood in hopes of having a feed for themselves.

"Time to go," I said to Boedi, now lying on his board and taking in the sun. "I think it's lunch time for our little friends."

We turned back towards the shore and paddled towards the bluff. The swell had grown since our arrival, approaching from the southeast and wrapping itself around the point into a section protected from the wind. This was producing beautiful four-foot peeling waves, ideal for a day on the sea.

It was a lot faster to paddle out from the north end, and we were eager to catch some rides. In a mad rush not to miss this session, we paddled hard back to the shore and quickly loaded the boards onto the roof of the car before driving over to the other side. A disappointing sight greeted us as we rounded the point. The waves, although in the right position, the right size, and with perfect winds, were too full. There was so much water in them that they weren't breaking, merely sliding past and dissipating into nothing closer to shore.

Unfortunate circumstances, yet not disheartened after our oceanic diving adventure, we decided to drive further up the coast to Rainbow Beach for lunch. As always, I grabbed the first round of beers as Boedi ordered potato wedges, a tradition dating back to as long as we could legally drink. Reflecting on the day, we recounted the experience each of us had had and agreed to make this a new tradition. The beers continued to flow and in a state of growing inebriation, I proclaimed that there was no better place on earth than the Sunshine Coast.

"That's a big call, mate. I love the coast too, but I don't know if it is the best place on earth," contested Boedi.

A debate erupted as I blindly defended my place of birth, citing its year-round great weather, relatively good surf, and proximity to the mountains, reminding Boedi of its great local vibe and diving, which he had just experienced first-hand.

Quick as a wink, Boedi defended his original position, agreeing that the Sunny Coast was great, very convenient and had a lot to offer. It did have good surf, but it didn't have great surf. It did have mountains, but they were not big mountains. It did have good diving, but not nearly as great as other places in the world. The Sunshine Coast was like that kid who was good at everything, but great at nothing. Everyone liked him, and he was always on the team, but he was never the first pick.

"Right, it has everything! It's extremely convenient and caters to everything we love doing. C'mon, Boedi, you and I have lived a dream growing up here, surfing all the time, going to waterfalls, diving, drinking great coffee, growing up with all the same people. It's not just what the Sunny Coast has to offer, but the past and memories that we share with this place."

Boedi hesitated, taking his time to sip the froth off his beer before turning his piercing eyes on me, as if he knew what he had to say would end the conversation altogether. Leaning back in his chair, a smile came over his face as he stated the obvious. "If it was the greatest place on earth, why would you want to go anywhere else?" He was hinting at the fact that I always tried to go away on trips, always tried to escape. Bastard, he's made a good point.

"Fine," I confessed, "either way, I am very happy to be spending my birthday here, on the Sunshine Coast, drinking a frothy to finish up a great day of diving."

"Cheers!" said Boedi, raising his glass.

I arrived home to a silent house, the doors and windows locked, and the lights turned off. Sandy was away and everything indicated that the day was over, but with all the excitement still pulsing through my veins, I couldn't think of a better way to release energy than to dance it off. Growing up with a father from South America, dancing had always been a part of me. Every night, my dad and I would dance, usually in the kitchen whilst cooking dinner, the rhythm of Latin music bouncing off the walls as my father led the way, showing me how to move with the music, dancing in sync with the beats.

Apart from my childhood kitchen, there were no Latin dance places on the entire coast. The few places available for any kind of dancing were the small clubs on Ocean Street, booming electronic music lacking style, to be danced to by people with no ability to move in step. It was expensive and hard to get into, and really not much fun. Recently however, a Spanish tapas bar had opened and a few nights a week they played all sorts of Spanish music: Salsa, bachata, reggeaton, merengue and so on. I hadn't gone yet, but as tonight was my birthday, it was the perfect night to let loose.

I tried to find something to wear. But as you have probably figured out by now, my style didn't exactly scream 'dresses' so I snuck into Sandy's room to see what she had. Sifting through her closet, I found a red singlet and a black skirt. Still undecided if this was 'sexy', but I liked the style and knew that it would go well with my converse shoes. Dressed and with hair washed, I was finishing up just as the taxi arrived, taking a shot of vodka before heading outside.

"Anyone else?" asked the taxi driver as I hopped into the front seat.

"Nah, mate, just me. Vamos."

"Really, I don't see that too often, usually you lot come in packs."

"Yeah, mate, well maybe I'm a lone wolf, just drive please," I said, trying hard to curb my sass.

Arriving at the club, I was surprised by the lack of people lined up at the door, causing second thoughts and I even considered just going home. However, it was only eight o'clock and I was not here for other people. I entered the club without hassle and because I was so early, I didn't have to pay a cover fee. 'Bonus,' I think to myself, 'I can afford an extra drink.'

My first vodka tonic disappeared in one go, only to immediately start another. I could feel the hypnotic rhythm of the music as the alcohol had its desired effect, relaxing me into a state of infatuation, moving slowly to the beat as I continued to sip down my second vodka. More people were arriving now, and seemingly within minutes, there were at least a hundred people in the club. The sudden influx cued the DJ that it was time to start, and he transitioned perfectly from the pre-recorded music to his live set, opening with his own mixed beat version of the song 'Bailando' by Enrique Iglesias, and creating a vibe like I have never experienced before.

The alcohol relaxed every nerve in my body, carrying my feet to the centre of the dancefloor. The music washed over me as I moved with perfect rhythm to the sounds and waves reverberating throughout the room; passion, absolute presence, the complete intoxication of the moment flooded over me as I moved oblivious to the people around me. Closing my eyes, I whipped my head back and forth, flinging my hair from side to side.

Clearly drawing attention, I found myself surrounded by a group of people, some dancing along, others admiring a talent not often seen in an Anglo, rhythmless place. Becoming very aware of my surroundings, self-consciousness sobered me up and not wanting to be watched like an animal in a zoo, I merged into the crowd. Seeing a guy who looked like he had some talent, I gave him that look which all women give. A look that said I had chosen him to dance with me. He immediately took the hint and approached, grabbing me around the waist and taking the lead without missing a beat, moving in rhythm with my hips and body.

Thirty minutes disappeared in what felt like a second, and soon I could feel myself sobering up. Time for another drink. I liked dancing with this guy and not wanting to lose him to the crowd, offered to buy him a round. One shot turned into three, and as the warmth of burning alcohol filled my stomach I was back, feeling alive and ready to dance the fuck out of this place. Grabbing the guy's arm, I dragged him back to the centre of the dance floor, taking careful sips of my cocktail as I danced along to the merengue music now blasting from the speakers.

Wanting to feel the rhythm of the music, I closed my eyes and a flashback to my dad's kitchen appeared, to my first time learning to dance. I was maybe four years old, wearing a yellow dress with white dots. It had no sleeves and was adorned by a wide sash which tied around the back in a bow, holding the top half still as the skirt section was free to billow up as I moved from side to side. I felt like Cinderella as I was directed by a large hand through each step. Laughing hysterically, I looked up into a round face bearing a smile of utmost kindness, green eyes staring past a large nose, observing his daughter in utter contentment.

My eyes shot open. "What the fuck was that?" The last thing I wanted to dwell on was a memory of my dad so I headed for the bar in need of another drink, followed keenly by my dance partner who was misinterpreting the sudden exit from the dance floor for something more. Too easy, I smiled to myself, he could pay for my vodka tonic and shot of tequila.

"That's better," feeling warm as the tequila relaxed my nerves and the shock of the flashback wore off. I grabbed the vodka tonic, now my fifth of the night and shot it down, before grabbing the guy by the waist and forcing him towards me. I pinned my hips to his as we moved in sync with the rhythm of the music. The DJ had slowed things down and was now playing bachata. We moved side to side, occasionally being thrown into a spin before stepping back into line. Bachata was by far my favourite style, the perfect mix between traditional dancing and free-spirited club music, as the songs were easy to dance to, allowing you to improvise and adapt with ease to your partner, your emotions and sexual tensions flowing freely. With artists like Juan Luis Guerra, Romeo Santos, and Melendi, the music had surged in popularity during my lifetime.

I closed my eyes again, letting the music take me, and was instantly transported back to my childhood kitchen. No more than a metre tall, I held onto my father as he guided me from side to side.

"One and two and, one and two and, one and two and, Mari, you are doing so well," my father encouraged as I moved my small feet back and forth across the tile floor. "This is called Bachata. It's very easy you see? As long as you stick to the beat, everything else works its way out."

"I keep messing up, Dad," I cried. "Can you help me?"

"Sure, mi amor, just stand on my feet."

I stepped up onto his shoes, which seemed giant in comparison to mine. Back and forth we continued, Dad moving my legs as he stepped, counting lightly as if to tell me a secret, all the while looking into the eyes of a daughter he loved more than anything in the world. This man seemed like a god to me. Staring up at him I felt very safe, certain he could do anything in the world. He was my superhero, my superman. I didn't know of anyone better, and he was teaching me how to dance. "Are you all right?" the guy asked, shaking my shoulder. I snapped back to reality. I had stopped dancing, staring forward into blank space.

"I'm fine, I just need a sec."

I rushed to the bathroom and found an open stall. Sitting on the toilet, I covered my face with my hands, breathing heavily. As I felt the room start to spin, I attempted to block out the memories that brought about so much guilt and loss. The sick feeling in my stomach was either from the emotional toll of reliving moments from my past or from the extreme quantity of alcohol I had just consumed. Without warning, I got the sudden urge to vomit, gagging as my throat closed in an effort to control the belching.

It didn't work and as I tilted my head towards the toilet bowl, vomit projected everything I had so foolishly taken in. Once it started it didn't stop, and for the next three minutes I continued this cycle with no end in sight. Eventually there was nothing left. There I was, half slumped over the toilet rim, arse on the floor and drool sneaking out of the side of my mouth. I couldn't get up. All I wanted was for this to end. I needed help, but I couldn't find the energy to call out. Out of sheer luck, I heard a voice from the stall next to me. I fumbled around to find my phone, sliding it under the wall towards the Good Samaritan's feet. "Ring Boedi!" I called, mumbling through tears. "I need Boedi!" I saw a hand grab the phone, and a moment later heard her speaking with someone. I began to fade in and out of consciousness, unable to make out what she was saying.

"I called Boedi," came the pleasant voice from the closet next door. "He said he is on his way."

"Thank you."

That was the last thing I remember saying before the door suddenly flew open. Without warning, I was lifted off the floor and carried out through the club. Blurred shadows of people stared pitifully as my feet dangled beneath me, toes scraping the sticky, alcohol covered floor, only to be taken outside and thrown onto the pavement. Grabbing the branch of a nearby potted tree I tried to hold myself steady. It felt like I was standing there for hours, swaying back and forth as people walked past without offering a word of help. I didn't care, fuck them. I just need to wait for…

"Mari! What the fuck, hello, Mari!"

Boedi's face was really close to mine. Why was he so close? I bet he wanted to kiss me. Well now was not the time. Just take me home. "Boedi! Hey, can you give me a lift? I'm not feeling well."

"For fuck's sake, c'mon, hold on to my shoulder. That's it, the car is just around the corner."

I tried my best to compose myself in a sexy way, only to trip and fall into the plant. "Fine, but can we stop at McDonald's on the way home? I'm starving!" That's all I remembered…

Breathe.

Chapter 4

The light was so bright. My eyes were tightly closed in fear of the impending brick of a hangover about to smash against my head. Any minute now, I was going to be taken to a world of pain, brought on by my own regrettable actions. The abomination affecting my body could only be worsened by the memories of last night.

In fear of the sting to come, I slowly fluttered my eyes open and lied there, waiting for them to adjust to the sunlight shining through the window. Sitting up in an effort to get out of bed, my head spun and the pain of a dehydration headache hit me like a sledgehammer. The relentless throbbing only made worse by fear of not remembering exactly how I left the club or knowing where I currently was. A breeze blowing through the window provided a momentary reprieve and my focus shifted to the room before me. There was a stool next to me with a glass of water and a half-eaten tortilla wrap lying on top.

The need to hydrate was insatiable and finishing the glass, I got out of bed in search for a refill. The house was silent. Somehow the hallways seemed familiar and with ease I was able to find the nearest bathroom. I looked like shit, the mirror reflecting a face of sunken eyes, pale skin and the lines of someone who hadn't slept in ten years. It was only when I immersed my face in a refreshing bath of cold water, revitalising my dehydrated skin and bringing some life back to my skeletal face that I realised where I was; in Boedi's house.

This process was repeated three times before I dried off and tiptoed to the kitchen. There I found Boedi making tea, his back to me and steam rising from the counter as he brewed his typical morning breakfast chai. I greeted him as I took my place at the table, expecting a hot beverage to be made for me as well. Boedi didn't respond, instead keeping his back to me as he continued to brew. Still no response as I greeted him again. Now I knew he was ignoring me. He turned around and leant against the counter to face me, placing a brewing cup of earl grey for me to drink. I heard him scoff under his breath. "You really don't remember?"

"No," I replied. "Not really, just bits and pieces."

"Are you fucking kidding me? You very easily could have died last night. What the fuck were you thinking? We had a great day yesterday, one of the best days ever. Was that not enough? Am I not enough? Are you so self-involved that you need to get fucked off your face to make the day worthwhile? When I found you, you were hanging off a tree, murmuring to yourself. You vomited three times on the way home. I had to force feed you. I should have taken you to the hospital. Please Mari, tell me how last night was worth getting alcohol poisoning."

"I'm sorry. I should have been more responsible; I didn't realise how much I had had to drink. I really am sorry. I don't know how to make it up to you."

"You don't owe me anything. Look mate, you need to stop drinking. Don't tell me you haven't been drinking a lot more lately. I can tell. You're not exactly hiding it, hanging out with those dickheads from the surf club. You're even getting drunk by yourself. You're going down a slippery slope and you need to stop before there is no coming back. Mari, you tested our friendship very seriously last night. If I didn't care about you, I wouldn't have come to help."

Feeling ashamed, I sat in silence as I finished the tea Boedi had given me, staring into my cup as I moved the teabag in circles with my spoon. All the while Boedi continued about his day as if I was not there at all. Pretty soon he left the kitchen, returning moments later to put on his shoes.

"I'm going to work," he said. "I don't want you here when I get back. And clean up after yourself before you go."

With that he left the house. I heard him start the car, back out of the driveway, and turn down the street. I did as I was told and went home. Emotionally unavailable to the rest of the world, I retreated to my room and lied on my bed, hoping I hadn't ruined everything with Boedi. I reassured myself, thinking he was just upset for the moment, a moment that would pass. We'd be fine.

Getting restless and not wanting to think too much about it, I grabbed my favourite longboard, a pacer, and headed down to the Alex Bluff. From the top of the hill, I could see that there were a few people out, but nobody I recognised. I paddled out through relatively small two footers and joined the line-up. Longboarding was such a fantastic way to relax on the water. It was easy to paddle, had longer rides, and allowed you to walk up and down the log, letting you be more creative and artistic in your style.

Turning, floating, and walking on the waves allowed me to escape and let go of the emotion of the day, providing the perfect release to the morning's stresses. Before I knew it, I was back in the moment, and focused on one thing and one thing only, the incoming wave. I grabbed the rails of my board and stood up slowly as the wave gained size under me, turning slightly and picking my line. The wave started to get ahead of me and I stepped forward, placing one foot in front of the other until I reached the tip.

Once at the front, I remained balanced on the wave, taking the opportunity to stand up as straight as a pencil, by placing both feet together on the front tip of the board. It was my favourite trick, and was both impressive and a bit show-off, but a move which gained respect given the skill required to execute it. Smiling to myself, I turned off the wave to paddle back toward the line-up, hearing the claps echo down from the old legends watching us from the top of the hill. My groove was quickly discovered amongst the waves and I cruised back to a state of self-satisfaction. The feelings and actions of the past few days were now behind me.

Boedi didn't call or text for five days. At first it didn't bother me. He was a busy guy with a lot on, however the surf was clean and of good quality all week. In all the time we have known each other, he had never failed to call me and talk about the waves or plan to meet up for a surf session. He couldn't possibly still be upset about last weekend. Surely he could have gotten over it by now.

Saturday rolled around and I still hadn't heard from him. Having called him multiple times already, I reckoned the only way to find out what was going on was to go to his house and figure it out. The fifteen-minute drive felt like days and although it was important to know the truth, I was worried that I wouldn't like his answer. Was it worth the risk of losing your closest friend? I didn't think I could afford to lose another loved one. My knuckles knocked on Boedi's door to no response. This time I rang the doorbell, still no response. Walking back to the car, the door suddenly opened and I turned around to see Boedi standing there. "Fuck me, you're alive? Why have you been ghosting me?"

"Well I was very upset mate. You really tested our friendship, and I wasn't sure what to do. I just thought it would be good to have a bit of space."

"So that's your solution? To test if you can live without me? I thought we were best mates? I don't know how many times I can say sorry. Can you really not forgive me? I guess I thought I was more important to you than that."

And that was it, the doubt filled question that every girl used to win an argument, but for good reason, because I meant every word of it.

"No. I don't want to lose you. You are way too important for that," Boedi stated. "I just want you to understand the serious implications your actions can have. You may not care about yourself, and in fact, I still don't understand what is going on with you, but you should care about how your actions affect the ones you love."

My heart sank. Here I was all huffed and puffed and about to give it to Boedi, only to now be on the other side of the lecture stick. It wasn't over.

"What if I wasn't there to help you that night?" he asked. "Do you even remember what happened? You could have ended up in the gutter and something serious could have happened. There are a lot of people that care about you. You shouldn't just live for yourself, because that is just fucking selfish. It's one thing to be independent. It's another to be alone."

We both stood there, silent. Boedi not looking away, emphasising the point he was trying to make. The silence was almost as powerful as the lecture itself, cementing his statements into certainty as I stood there in humble acceptance of what was said. I was like a dog with its tail between its legs who knew it had done something wrong.

"Now come on in, I'm just making some toasted sandwiches and you look hungry."

The lunch was impeccable, every bite filled with relief and the assurance of an amended friendship. I did burn my tongue, but shit, nothing was perfect. We made a second round of toasted sandwiches and took them out to the back deck to enjoy the sunshine. Boedi continued to watch me, analysing me for some reason and I could feel his eyes following me as I ate. It wasn't not the most comfortable feeling.

"So," said Boedi casually, leaning back in his chair as if he were some sort of shrink. "What's really going on with you?"

"What do you mean?"

"C'mon mate, don't beat around the bush, you can just tell me. I'm an open ear of confidentiality." He raised three fingers into the air, demonstrating the Boy Scout sign to show he was trustworthy. I imagined he was still talking about what happened the other night, and I explained that it had been a long time since I had moved to any real dance music, that there were just no good Latin dance places on the coast.

"That's not what I am talking about," responded Boedi. "All year you have been drinking more frequently, you're a bit distant sometimes, and you blow up quickly these days. I mean a few weeks ago, you told someone to go fuck themselves just because they assumed you were indigenous instead of Chilean."

"Yeah but I'm not indigenous," I snapped. "I'm Australian, plain and simple. I just have Chilean heritage."

"This is exactly my point. You just get your back up over nothing at times. The old mate was just asking a question, and honestly, it shouldn't matter."

"I have been drinking more. That's probably making me testier. No need to worry anymore though. I think I've learnt my lesson. I'm not going to drink like that ever again."

Boedi stared at me again, analysing my facial expression to see if I was hiding the truth. He was very good at this, but I tried to act normal and sincere as I pushed the real reasons for my change in character to the deepest part of my being. I could tell he didn't believe me, but he didn't say anything, merely shrugging and grabbing the last half of his sandwich. He reassured me of his trust, licking the crumbs off the tips of his fingers as I started to clean the table. Boedi came to his feet to help, taking my plate to the kitchen before seeing me out to the front door. "Just know, even though you're aware of how I feel about your drinking, don't ever not call me when you need help, okay?"

"Deal."

Arriving home, I felt much better than when I left. I stated in victory under my breath, "I've got me mate back," the emotional relief of the afternoons' events falling off my shoulders like a perpetual weight. In a great mood, and now with an afternoon to myself, I couldn't think of anything better than to have a soak in the tub before relaxing with a book on the back deck.

I drew a hot bath and quickly undressed, slipping my naked body into the soothing, soapy bubbles. The water almost spilt over the side as I took a deep breath and let myself sink down, immersing myself completely, letting my head submerge beneath the bubbles. Almost instantly I could feel my face soften as it moisturised in the solution. Eyes closed, I could easily fall asleep, almost floating above the bottom of the tub.

Suddenly, I found myself underwater, not in the bath, but in the blue abyss of the same unknown ocean reef as previously. I was just floating there, less relaxed than last time, my heart already racing as I tried to understand my surroundings. I held still, not wanting to disturb the scene around me. Fish were swimming in all directions and they appeared to be in distress as well. Once again, this scene felt so alive. How could it be? How could I have the same recurring dream, yet one that always felt more and more real with every occurrence?

As I took a closer look at my surrounding sea creatures, it seemed there was nothing normal about their actions. 'Maybe it was me,' I thought, believing that a foreigner entering into their home had caused a chain reaction of instinctive concern. A fish, maybe a tuna, came up to my face, pausing in front of me to investigate. Quite large, its beady eyes popped out of its silvery, scaly body as it stared at me, trying to figure out what I was. I stared back, unable to look away as its gaze trapped me in a curious hypnosis. I tilted my head to the right, and it moved right. I tilted my head to the left and the fish moved left.

'How bizarre,' I thought, continuing to move my head back and forth, dancing with the fish in a synchronised movement that affected both. I didn't take my eyes off his, and for a moment, I thought I felt his emotion. Sorrow? Familiarity? Fear? It was hard to tell if I was looking in the fish's eyes or at my own reflection.

My chest started to convulse, breaking my concentration as the urge to breathe became overwhelming. I could feel the pressure building in my chest and desperately tried to control my emotions so as to not freak out. I looked up, my diaphragm screaming as it tried to breathe. I could see white clouds above me as waves folded and crashed back into the sea, billowing in beauty, but meaning death if I couldn't pass through them to the surface. I tried to swim towards the safety above but found myself not rising. Why couldn't I move? My chest had stopped convulsing, but the need for oxygen still desperately tried to force my mouth open. In my struggle I had gained an audience as the fish from earlier returned to view the spectacle. They watched as I struggled to breathe, and like boys on a fishing trip, got excited as the sea took me back.

Bam! Out of nowhere a shark came from my right and ate the fish, snatching them out of the water in the blink of an eye. The shock woke me from my trance and I jumped out of the bathwater, smashing my forehead on the tap in the process. "AAAAAHH!"

The pain was instant. Like a lightning bolt, a hot fiery stabbing pain ran through my entire body, causing me to fall back into the water, grabbing my head with my hands and writhing in pain. Sandy rushed into the bathroom. She halted at the door, dumbstruck as she looked upon my naked body now half out of the tub as I tried not to vomit on myself, blood pouring onto the floor through my right hand as it refused to let go of my forehead.

"Oh my gosh! Oh my gosh! Oh my gosh!" gasped Sandy, now on her knees next to me, panicking and trying to figure out what to do. "Are you all right?" she asked, unable to find any consoling words that might help.

Through gritted teeth and tears, I responded. "No. Fuck! I think I need to go to the hospital.
Can you help me?"

"Yes, of course! Let me get some towels."

Sandy sprinted into action, rushing out of the bathroom to find anything that might help. I fell out of the tub, landing on the cold tiles, folding myself into the foetal position and doing the only thing I could think of to help my situation, focus on my breath.

Returning with a stack of towels, the first half she dumped on the floor, mopping up the bloody water and providing a comfortable spot to sit. She wrapped another towel around me and helped me dry off in silence. She may have thought that she wasn't helping much, barely able to keep herself together enough to take charge of the situation, but right now she was nothing short of a miracle. "It's going to be okay."

"I know, thank you," I responded.

"I wasn't talking about you."

We stood up, me cupping a towel to my head with as much pressure as I could bear. Still naked, I made my way to my room and found the loosest pair of tracksuit pants and hoody I could find, dressing myself before heading for the car.

"Maybe we should call an ambulance," suggested Sandy, worried and not wanting to be responsible if something happens.

"No, I'm not dying. Besides, I don't want to waste their time when they could be helping someone who actually needs it, I'll just have to take a concrete pill and harden the fuck up, but can you please drive fast?"

With that, Sandy floored it, going as fast as she felt safe towards the new Sunshine Coast University Hospital. It was by far the longest fifteen minutes of my life and I just wanted the pain to stop, but I could feel a bump the size of a tennis ball forming under the towel and I hoped it was not as bad as it felt.

Arriving at hospital, we made our way to the semi-empty emergency department where we were seen immediately. I was relieved at the speed of care provided, as typically I wouldn't be classed as a priority and would be made to wait a long time. Tonight was my lucky night.

With the pain medication still to take effect, the wound was about as bad as it felt. Nine stitches, a high price to pay for taking a bath. The bad news was that the doctor said if I played by the rules, I probably wouldn't get a scar, but that meant no surfing for two weeks. What was a scar anyway? I'd be like Harry Potter, just cooler. Sandy had disappeared, but returned, her hands filled with snacks extracted from the vending machine down the corridor. Numbed of consciousness as the medicine kicked in, I didn't think I was high, but I felt fantastic. "Sandy, you're a lifesaver," I said whimsically, grabbing a bag of chips and wolfing them down in one ravenous move. "Guess what? I am all stitched up and good to go."

I shot Sandy a wink in an attempt to assure her that I'd be okay. Having known me for a long time now, Sandy had an acute ability to see through the smoke screen of bullshit that came from my mouth on a regular basis. We left the hospital and made our way to Low Tide, by far the coolest coffee shop on the coast, tucked away in the small town of Marcoola. Looking over the coast from the street side of the beach, its overhanging wooden rafters allowed you to enjoy the beach lifestyle whilst nestled in the comfort of a quiet, local café.

"You can't go surfing. You heard what the doctor said," warned Sandy.

"No, the doctor said if I go surfing, it won't heal properly, and I'll most likely have a nasty scar. It's different."

"Please don't go surfing, Mari. I know you love being in the water, but can you not take a week or so off to let your wound heal?"

There wasn't really a debatable response to that. She was right, I could take two weeks off for something like this. However, just for the record, I didn't want to. Instead, I offered a proposition, asking slyly if it counted if I were on the water rather than in it. Sandy accused me of twisting her words in an attempt to have a scapegoat should I go surfing, and crossing her arms, informed me of her disappointment, feeling used and believing our friendship to be above that.

There was no trickery, no sly play of words, and I would never cross my friend such as she was suggesting. I was being sincere in my subtle attempt to spark interest from my coffee companion. I meant it when I said 'on' the water, divulging my newfound plan to purchase an old sail boat and fix it up to be sea worthy again. I'd need to find the money but think about it. With my head still on the mend and restricted from water activities I could do repairs on the boat, and then when I was cleared by the doctor, I'd be able to travel wherever I wanted to find surf. Sounded like the dream, right?

"Wow, you must have hit your head hard with a crazy idea like that. You don't have any money, and boats are expensive," said Sandy. "Do you even know how to sail?"

"I'll figure it out. It doesn't seem too hard, my dad learnt by himself. A few years ago, I actually tried to buy a boat with my dad and fix it up."

"Really? I didn't know that. Why didn't you do it?"

"Dad didn't want to buy a boat. We always talked about going around the world looking for surf, but when it came to sailing, he always got upset and refused."

We sat there deep in thought, savouring the last few drops of our coffee. Sandy excused herself to use the toilet, and in my solitude, I found myself looking aimlessly out to sea. My mind had drifted to my dad, and the constant arguments we had about buying the boat. Like a dream you barely remembered, I could never quite figure out his reasoning. All I could do was remember him.

My dad and I had always talked about travelling the world, surfing the best waves, and finding new breaks. Spending years dreaming about the trip, a journey with no end, I had hoped it would be the start of a never-ending life of adventure, cultural enlightenment, and self-actualisation.

As my ideas grew, and new places came to mind, I would research them endlessly. Everything from awesome breaks, the best time of year to go, where to stay, and so on. All of this I kept in a massive scrapbook, an ever-growing collection of aspirations. One day, I hoped to live out this dream, taking a page out of my own book, and filling my head with a bounty of unforgettable memories. Everywhere my dad and I wanted to go was connected to the sea, so it seemed obvious that we would take a boat, learning to sail as we went, and having the opportunity to travel wherever we wanted, on our own schedule, living the experience twenty-four hours a day, seven days a week, for years on end.

This was where dad and I disagreed. He had the same dream, but was completely opposed to sailing. I didn't understand it. Wasn't it he who sailed here from Chile when he was younger? Wasn't it he who used to own a boat? How could someone with those experiences, with that past and knowledge, and with so much love for the ocean, not want to sail?

The trip was a constant topic of conversation. Every few months we would go on long walks along a local stretch of beach called the 'North Shore'. Located on the northern side of the Maroochy River, little development, no traffic, and very dog friendly, it was a local's dream getaway only fifteen minutes up the road.

Like all beaches on the eastern seaboard, the North Shore faced the Pacific. Halfway between Sydney and the Great Barrier Reef, it was a much-frequented path for many sailboats and I had the habit of making sure to point them out as we walked, always making a cheeky comment to my dad. "Wouldn't it be great to bob up and down like a cork, wind in your face and drinking a nice cold beer as the sun sets?"

"Yeah, Mari, almost as nice as watching the sunset from the patio or on the beach. No, the beach actually sounds better."

"Why are you so opposed to sailing? Logically, it makes the most sense for what we want to do, and you know how to sail?"

"Enough Mari, I am not going to live on a sail boat again. It's just not going to happen, so can you please drop it?"

By the look on his face, I could tell he was serious, expressing that just the thought of it haunted him like a bad dream, seared into his frontal lobe like a record playing over and over again. I wondered what could have caused such a surge of unrelenting fear, a fear to repeat events from his past that although ultimately led him to the life which he loves so dearly, but one that if given the chance, he would never repeat.

We walked in silence for the next twenty minutes, the need to know the truth becoming unbearable. I thought dad and I told each other everything. Now I was starting to realise that there was so much that I didn't know. Arriving at the car, I found myself unable to hold it in any longer. "Dad, can we go get a coffee?"

"Sure," he replied

We drove to Low Tide. As always, I ordered a flat white for myself and a long black for Dad. Returning to the table, I placed the coffees in front of their respective drinkers and having planned my questions ahead of time, turned to start my interrogation. In true fashion however, my dad beat me to the punch. "So, I bet you're trying to find out why I hate sailboats?"

"Err, yeah. I mean, it just doesn't make sense. I feel like there is something you are not telling me."

I stared at him, determined to find out, expecting every excuse under the sun: Boats were expensive, I get seasick, etc. What I didn't expect for my dad to say is that he left Chile to escape communism and that he nearly died on the journey, more than once being caught in a storm. He stated simply that if it wasn't for the Australian navy, he most certainly would have perished.

"Are you ready to go home?" asked Sandy having returned from the bar.

I snapped out of my daydream, and standing up to leave, immediately fell back into my chair.

"Are you okay?"

"Yeah, I think so, still a bit dizzy I reckon. Can you give me a hand to the car?"

Making our way home, I easily drifted off to sleep, exhausted from the commotion of the day and wishing it had ended on a better note. For two whole weeks, I couldn't surf. I couldn't even go swimming. The best I could do was wade up to my waist, but what was the point of that? I think the term 'a fish out of water' would not only be extremely cliché, but also quite accurate. To keep myself occupied, I picked up extra shifts at work, watched the boys surf at Point Cartwright, and drank lots of coffees, mostly with Sandy, but every so often, Boedi would be keen for some caffeine.

Slowly, the pain in my head subsided, the swelling disappearing as the cut started to heal. By the end of the first week, I was already pulling out stitches and became hopeful I'd get wet sooner than expected. With all the extra shifts I was picking up, I made enough money in two weeks to give myself some savings, something I hadn't had in a long time, excluding surf trip money, which was a necessity, obviously. I was somewhat surprised at my fortune and reminded that you never know how one event could affect the next, reminding me of a story I was once told by a philosophy teacher.

'There was a Chinese man who lost his horse one day. All of his neighbours came around in the evening, and they said, 'Well, that's too bad', to which the Chinese man responded, 'Maybe.' The next day, the horse returned, bringing with it six wild horses to be tamed. In the evening, all of the neighbours came around and they said, 'Well, that's very lucky', to which the Chinese man responded, 'Maybe.' The universe is very complex, and it's impossible to think that one event will lead to another. Sometimes, what we think is bad luck, in fact is a blessing.'

Finally, after nearly two painstakingly long weeks, the last stitch popped out and with it, permission to return to the sea. Waking up to see the tiny blue piece of string sitting innocently on my pillow, I didn't even hesitate. Like a loaded spring, I launched out of bed and ran to the car, my board already strapped to the roof in anticipation for this day and wasting no time, I sped straight to the Alex bluff, not even bothering to put on shoes.

No waves. No wind. Flat as a lake. I didn't care. I dressed quickly, surely giving someone a nude show in my haste, and made my way down the beach as fast as I could. I felt like a puppy who had waited all day for its owner to come home.

I ran toward the shoreline, transitioning easily from a beach run to a glide over the calm water. Sitting up on my knees, I paddled, and kept paddling, as hard as I could. Big, strong strokes, carrying me out to sea as I sped across the surface. I paddled harder and faster, to the point of maximum effort. After ten minutes, I stopped paddling and sat up. In a rush of adrenaline, I couldn't help but yell out.

"YEEEEEEEWWWWWWW!" I screamed, raising my arms in victory and letting myself fall sideways into the water. I held my breath for as long as I could, which in this moment was about three seconds. With a mixture of emotion and salt water making me crazy, I resurfaced to yell in my best Scottish accent, "FREEEDOOO!" mocking Mel Gibson from his movie 'Braveheart'.

It's funny how the moments you remember are nearly always unexpected events. At the time, they seem insignificant compared to other parts of life, but through reliving the experience, it becomes obvious that it was that moment which helped define who you have become. That first day back on the water stuck with me as a symbol of emancipation, letting myself go to a place that carried me to nirvana.

Breathe.

It was now May, about a month after the incident and the scar was almost gone. It was as if it had never happened in the first place and I should have been elated but during this month, I found it hard to smile, unable to feel happy and even harder to fake it. May was when my father died. Every year, I thought it would get easier, that I wouldn't think about it as much or that maybe I'd be fortunate enough to forget, but it never happened. I didn't know if that was normal. The only other person I knew who had been through such a personal ordeal was my dad and he never forgot, always getting grumpy for weeks surrounding what he called 'Hermano Memorial Day'. Ironically, he had passed his curse onto me, and he wasn't even around for me to blame.

Although able to surf to my heart's content now that I had healed, I hadn't shortened my shift load at the surf shop. The money was too good, and I took every extra shift available, even managing to convince some naïve kid that I would pay him twenty dollars to let me take his shift. He saw easy coin, but I saw even more money.

On the anniversary of my father's passing I always visited his headstone at the top of the Alex bluff to show my respects and clean up the area, occasionally planting colourful flowers. Additionally, and most importantly, I took this opportunity to speak to him and catch him up on my life. My father wasn't buried as his ashes were spread in the ocean, for all those who come from the sea must return to her. The community had come together to raise money, using the funds to create a memorial at his favourite place to watch the ocean. It was their way of honouring him, and giving me a place to visit when I felt the need.

It was significant that the entire community showed up to his funeral, to pay their respects. Those with surfboards paddled and those without borrowed canoes, all coming together in front of the Alex Surf club to form the biggest circle I had ever seen. The local priest came to give his blessing, as did the head of the surf club. No words were spoken by me, instead saying what I needed to silently as I spread his ashes over the surface of the clear, pacific water.

"Hey, boss, can I have the rest of the afternoon off? I need to visit my dad's memorial."

"No," he responded. "You'll just have to go another day. If he were sick, then maybe, but your father is dead, he isn't going anywhere."

In a fury, I lashed out, without thinking of the implications, emotion taking over, with practicality left as an afterthought. "You know what? Go fuck yourself. How dare you be so disrespectful? I'm going."

"How dare he say such a thing?" I screamed to myself as I got into the car, hitting my hand against the roof, the sharp pain not releasing any of my anger. How could he think so little of my dad? My father was everything he wasn't, and he should want to be more like him.

I couldn't help it. In my anger there was sorrow, and with sorrow, came tears. I arrived at the carpark crying. As I walked over to his headstone, I tried to make myself as presentable as possible, not wanting to show my sadness so that my dad could still be proud. It didn't work and sitting against his memorial, I began to confess like a sinner to a priest, telling him how I felt lost, how I didn't know where my life was going, and that every year, I thought it would get easier, but it only got harder. "I don't know what to do, and I don't know anyone else I can ask. Please tell me what to do." Silence.

"Please, Dad, I beg you. Please show me a sign, anything."

Silence.

"Answer me!" I yelled, kicking the headstone.

Still no response. I was left feeling lonelier than ever before, and the last place I knew where to find solace had left me even more hopeless. I walked back to my car, head bowed, unresponsive to my surroundings. Numbly I drove off, and noticing a bottle shop, didn't hesitate to pull in. In the bottle shop, going straight to the back without being seen, I grabbed a bottle of bourbon and a six-pack of Canadian Club.

"Are you all right?" asked the cashier as I paid for the bottles.

"Mind your own business," I snapped as I handed over the money.

"Whatever mate, just trying to help."

As I walked back to the car, and before even opening the door, I cracked the lid on the bourbon, taking a long swig, alcohol dripping down my neck. Sitting in the car, I took another long drink before starting the engine and driving off in the direction of home.

The drive took longer than expected and with it came sobriety, the numbness starting to dissipate as the emotions returned even stronger than before. Snatching a look into the rear-view mirror, I was horrified at what I saw: Weakness. Was I that weak? Was I that worthless? Did no one care?

The first can of Canadian Club was drained in one go, cracking another one as I pulled into the driveway. The hinges creaked as I swung the car door open and stumbled out, the alcohol seeming to have found my blood stream and sense of balance. Standing up, I made a half-arsed attempt to close the car door behind me, only to miss and let my arm swing around in mid-air. My state only made me think less of myself, but I miraculously found my way to my room and slammed the door closed behind me, shutting myself off from the outside world.

Losing count of the number of drinks I'd consumed, I opened another, this one spilling down my shirt. Pathetic, I was nobody. I didn't even know who I was. A tear ran down my cheek, but I quickly wiped it away. Just standing there, staring at myself, self-loathing, taking drink after drink. It was like a challenge. If I turned away, stopped staring for one second, I would come to realise how weak I was, how lonely, how unloved I felt, yet as I continued to stare, I began to feel these things anyway. 'Who does this bitch think she is?' I thought to myself. 'What have you got to show for yourself? A couple of shit boards and nobody to come home to?'

Bringing the bottle to my lips, I didn't stop until the last drops had fallen into my mouth. As the alcohol burned down my chest and into my stomach, I could feel the warmth and destruction at the same time. Its effects were almost immediate and I started swaying from side to side, so much so that I had to lean over and hold myself against the wall. The mirror was right next to me now, and I continued to stare at it sideways. Drool hit my foot, but I couldn't really control my mouth, so I let it go.

Motionless for what seemed like an eternity, although, it was probably only five minutes, maybe ten, I began to come out of the cloud of semi consciousness that gave me the appearance of the walking dead. The more clearly I began to think, the stronger the anger became. Anger at the world and that fucking chick in the mirror. "Leave me alone!!!" I screamed, slamming my fist against the mirror, glass breaking under the force of my hand. "AAAAHHHH! I can't take it anymore! I've had it!"

I picked up the lamp and threw it at the wall as hard as I could. It smashed into pieces. It was my flatmate's, but I didn't care. 'Why would I? Fuck her. She's spying on me, I know it. Always creeping around quietly, seeing what I am up to, and asking me questions. Who does she think she is? She's a nobody.'

Looking around, I saw my longboard leaning against the bedside table. Like a beacon in the fog I was drawn to it, grabbing it in a fury, and in a spin that resembles a kung fu move from one of those old Chinese movies, I slammed the longboard against the wall. I struck again, and again, repeatedly until I couldn't support its weight any longer. Collapsing in a ball on the floor, the tears started to flow.

Crying, weeping, yelling, I was so alone. Everything I held dear was gone, and everything I ought to become was lost.

So engrossed in my own feelings, I gave no notice to my surroundings or the thought that the effects of my actions would draw the attention of others. As it turned out, constantly screaming and smashing shit against a wall was a cause for alarm, and when all of a sudden, I felt myself being picked up off the floor, I was shocked back into the present. "Mari, I am Officer Jacobs. Are you okay?"

Sandy must have called the cops out of fear. Maybe she thought I would hurt myself or do something I would regret. Either way, she was scared and responded the only way anyone in this situation would.

The officer lifted me off the floor with a firm grip and as I writhed with all my strength to escape his clutches, I heard the soothing voice of a stranger, offering his sincere assistance to make sure I was okay. "It's all right, stand up. Let's go get you some help," said Officer Jacobs.

"No! Leave me alone, I don't want your help," I replied, trying to make myself heavy.

I was exhausted, and with nothing to hold on to, Officer Jacobs lifted me into his arms with ease and carried me outside, placing me in the back seat of his car. "I don't want to go to jail, I just want to die. Leave me alone! I don't want to do this anymore." I was desperate now. I just wanted out. Out of this situation, out of my feelings, out of my life. I was broken, the pieces scattered across an ocean of loss and nostalgia, with no way of knowing how to collect the pieces.

"You're not going to jail," replied Officer Jacobs, "I am taking you to a place where you can be looked after, a place to help. It's going to be okay."

Giving in, I lied down as I was taken to God knows where. For about 30 minutes, we drove, the twists and turns of the drive easing me to drowsiness, quietly sobbing to myself as my eyes became heavier and heavier, eventually falling away into a dreamless slumber.

Breathe...

The smell of salt in the air, the wind blowing the scent of seaweed in through the window from the ocean. Eyes shut, I could hear the ocean moving, and waves crashing against the shoreline as the heat of the sun was relieved only by sea breeze encircling the room. Feeling like I'd slept for days, I slowly became more conscious, and sensing that I was somewhere familiar, I opened my eyes and was immediately blinded by the midday sun, forcing me to squint so my pupils could adjust to the light.

"How are you feeling?" came a familiar voice.

"Boedi, is that you? Where am I? What happened? Last thing I remember, I was on my way to the police station."

"You've been asleep for a long time, about 16 hours," said Boedi, entering the room and sitting on the end of the bed. "I met the cop at the station. He didn't really know what to do with you, and you were fast asleep. I said I could take care of you and that you would be all right. I figured it would be good to get out of town, somewhere quiet to clear your head, so I brought you to my parents' beach house."

Now more aware of my surroundings, I looked around and it suddenly made sense why I felt I was somewhere familiar. As children, Boedi and I would visit his grandparents often, using their house as our secret surf and adventure spot. His grandma and grandpa knew we came over only because they had a great home that sat right on the beach, but they enjoyed our company none the less, and were amused watching us go on 'adventures'.

"I didn't know that you still had this house," I stated, yawning so wide that my eyes began to water.

"Yeah, my parents couldn't bring themselves to sell it after my grandparents passed. They just love this place so much," Boedi replies, sitting on the end of the bed. "I'm going to get a coffee, do you want one?"

"The usual."

Boedi left the room and I pulled myself out of bed. Walking over to the French doors, I pulled the lace curtains back, revealing the most spectacular view of the sea. The house sat perched atop an ocean bluff and I could see across the open ocean for miles. Facing east, the house witnessed the most stunning sunrises, and was occasionally visited by a passing whale, which never hesitated to show off with a splash as it made it way north to give birth.

From a seat on the step leading out onto the balcony. I felt my head throbbing as I tried to sift through fragmented memories. What I did remember was a feeling of horrendous depression, of anger, and giving up. Hopefully no one was hurt during my rampage, but waking up two hours from home didn't exactly give me a lot of confidence.

Boedi seemed to take his time, but I was grateful for the solitude. It was peaceful here, and with the wind blowing ever so gently, the nightmares of the previous night became less burdensome, at least for the time being.

"Hey, sorry I took so long, traffic was a fuckin nightmare," said Boedi handing me a coffee as he sat down next to me. "I want to talk about what happened."

"I know, I got a little carried away. I promise it won't happen again."

"Last night was the final straw. You need to deal with this. You need help."

Hanging my head in shame, I tried to hide the tears forming in the corners of my eyes. Vulnerable, a feeling with which I was not familiar and which I did not like. My ability to shove the truth down inside and put on a strong face was getting harder, and I was reluctant to let myself go in the presence of someone I trusted so much. "I can handle it," I said, wiping my eyes quickly and looking straight ahead, as if nothing were wrong.

"No you can't. You're a train wreck. Look mate, I'm only going to tell it to you straight. I care about you and you don't need any fluffy bullshit, but I can't help you if you don't acknowledge that you are struggling and that you need help and really try your hardest to overcome the loss of your dad. Otherwise, you will never have a real chance at getting better. I think you have been struggling with not having him here. I think you are a little lost, you're lonely."

Boedi was right, I did need to find my way. If a car was coming towards you, do you stand still and get hit or move out of the way and save yourself? Why not step to the side with your thumb out, just to see where life will take you?

"Look mate, you're right, I have been feeling out of sorts for a while now, but I don't know how to fix it?"

"I have an idea!" shouted Boedi, jumping up with excitement and bringing a whole new energy to the conversation. "You don't know where you are unless you know where have come from."

"That's the dumbest cliché I have ever heard. What are you talking about?"

And without another word, Boedi left the room.

Breathe.

Chapter 5

My heart raced as I woke up to realise the plane had started its descent to land where it all began. Chile. Although my family came from this country, I could not have felt more like a fish out of water. I fastened my seatbelt and ensured my seat was in the upright position when a group of students behind me started screaming. "Say Achay EEE!" yelled one lad.

"Chi!" screamed the rest.

"Elay AY!"

"Lay!"

"Chi Chi Chi! Lay Lay Lay! Viva Chile!!!" they all screamed together. Three times they repeated this war cry. They were chanting their country's' motto, and it reminded me of all the drunks at the footy matches back home. This was the introduction to my past. Welcome to Chile.

Entering the airport, I was greeted and kindly directed to the customs agent in charge of making sure my visa and passport were accurate, before officially stamping me into the country. With confidence, I handed over my documents only to be met with an expression of confusion as the agent looked at my passport, then to me. He did it again, now causing me to be concerned that something may be wrong with my visa. "You are Australian?" he questioned.

"Yes."

"But you look Chilean, and you have a Chilean last name?" he asked again.

Annoyed, I explained that my dad was Chilean, but I was Australian as obviously demonstrated by my passport. He began to speak to me in Spanish, ignoring what I had just said. Getting upset now, I stated as clearly as possible that I didn't speak Spanish, and I didn't appreciate his assumption that I did, just because of my appearance.

"You gringos are so rude, no wonder no one likes you," he scorned, stamping my passport and shoving it back to me.

Picking up my bags from the baggage area, I made my way to the exit when out of nowhere I was swarmed by what seemed like hundreds of Chilean drivers asking me to ride in their taxi. Each of them with no concept of personal space, they stood directly in my way to tell me that they were the cheapest, fastest, and would get me exactly where I needed to go.

Overwhelmed to say the least, I would later learn that you had to be firm and decisive when dealing with situations like these, to block out everyone except the person with whom you were speaking. Without being disrespectful, but putting everything in order, and achieving what you were trying to accomplish. However, being my first time dealing with this situation, none of the above happened.

It all became too much, and after the eighth or ninth person shoved his demanding face into mine, I just said 'okay'. Fortunately for him, I hadn't seen the bus that costs three dollars to get to the main bus terminal, nor the private taxis that cost 20 dollars. At the end of the day, I suppose it was my fault. I was the 'rich' gringo that knew no better, and the taxi driver could get away with charging me 70 bucks upon arrival at the bus terminal.

Boedi had given me directions on every step required to get from the airport to my grandma's house in Copcecura. Incredibly impressed, I noticed that he had put in so much effort and detail as to call and converse with my extended family that neither of us had ever met. They had given him clear directions on everything I needed before and after I arrived and had stated that I may stay for as long as I wanted, the longer the better. Perplexed by this sign of hospitality, I wondered how they could be so welcoming.

'I don't deserve this,' I thought as I sat in the back of the most expensive taxi in the world. 'How could they be so kind to a stranger? They knew my father, not me. What if they didn't like me? I mean I was not exactly the kind of girl someone showed off?' Thoughts like these continued to run through my head. I suppose if I was constantly questioning the situation, I wouldn't have to face everything I was trying to escape from.

"*Estamos aqui*," said the driver suddenly, drawing me back to reality.

"*Si*," I responded in Spanish, hoping that the driver would have the same thought as the customs agent and give me a discount.

"Seventy dollars please," he said smirking, "Cash only."

Getting out of the taxi, I pulled out the instructions given by Boedi.

'*Go to the ticket counter just inside the terminal at the front. There you will see multiple lines, each marked with a town. Get into the line that says Concepcion. It will cost about 20 dollars. Just say Concepcion and hand over the money to receive your ticket. On the ticket, it will give you a bus port number. Go there and wait. When a bus turns up, it will say Concepcion in the window. If it doesn't say Concepcion, it is not your bus, so be careful. Do not leave the bus port or you may miss your ride. The buses aren't exactly on schedule.*'

Following the directions exactly, I found my way onto the bus and was happy to see that I managed to score a window seat. For the next seven hours we made our way through the country, stopping in each town to pick up and drop off passengers. Everything seemed archaically beautiful, not up to the times, but somehow exuded character. At every stop, middle-aged women boarded the bus, selling pastries from their wicker baskets. For 50 cents, you could receive the most delicious homemade croissant.

Having zero ability to speak Spanish or what sounded like a strange version of the Spanish I had heard previously, I took full advantage of the window seat, admiring the landscape and the varied complexities contained within. On leaving Santiago, I was greeted with dirty, run down outer suburbs. I was used to travelling to impoverished countries in Indonesia, but this had its own style. Mud and old brick houses, all linked by a maze of rusted tin roofs. Lacking the infrastructure and money of the inner city, the rundown buildings and sparse streets gave a greater view of what the landscape was really like. It was clear that Santiago sat on the southern end of the Atacama Desert, separating Chile's north and south and was blanketed by a mist of smog caught in the nook of the Andes Mountains. The landscape changed rapidly. Heading south, you drive through a corridor of mountains, the grand Andes to the east, and the coastal mountain range to the West. Between them, one main highway extended through the entire country, surrounded by an extension of vineyards producing Malbec wines, for which Chile had become famous.

The landscape changed so quickly here. The further south we went, the greener the landscape became. The only constant being the Andes Mountains. Extending more than 4,000 kilometres north to south, these stunning mountains bordered the entire country. Visible from every part of Chile, it was an iconic feature in which the Chilean people held great pride. It was recounted in their songs, has forged its way into their culture, and made up an important part of the Chilean way or life. It reminded me of my connection to the ocean, and for the first time, I felt myself connecting with my past.

After five hours, the bus arrived in the city of Chillan, the last stop before Concepcion and only an hour and a half remaining in my drive to an unknown home. Excitement grew as the feeling of this adventure became real, my previous fears receding to the back of my mind. Out of nowhere, I heard my name. 'It must be a mistake,' I thought, as it was hard to decipher this weird language the Chileans thought was Spanish. I was never sure what they were saying, nor was I expecting anyone to call my name. "Mari, are you on the bus?" I heard again.

I sat up straight to see a middle-aged man standing by the driver looking down the aisle, scanning all of the faces. He was different from the others I had seen so far: Wearing a black jumper, slacks, and with a tidy haircut, it was obvious he was wealthier than most. "Aqui," I said, raising my hand to let him know where I was, but not wanting others to know I was a foreigner. Who wanted a repeat of the taxi situation? "Ah perfect." He sounded English, and it confused me as he made his way down to my row, taking the seat next to me, and kissing me on the cheek.

"Wow, mate, what the fuck?" I exclaimed, retracting from a cultural exchange of which I was not accustomed.

"Pardon me. It is how we say hello in Chile. My name is Rodrigo. I am an old friend of your dad. I was in Chillan for the day and am on my way to your grandma's house. I thought I would accompany you, and make sure you found your way."

"Oh, okay. Err thank you so much." How kind. I would never in a million years have expected such selflessness. "You are the first person that hasn't harassed me since I got here," I said, attempting small talk with a complete stranger, who in these foreign circumstances had just become my first Chilean friend. "Are there more like you?"

"Haha welcome to Chile. It has a lot of sides you know, and if you are coming from Australia, this will all be very strange. But yes, Chileans are generally nice people. You just have to learn how to interact with them."

Bloody hell, who wouldn't be mates with this guy. For the next hour and half, we discussed an array of topics. Rodrigo spoke mostly about Chile; the history, the language, and differences between countries. It was extremely insightful and proved you could learn more from an honest conversation than in any classroom or tutorial.

"Chileans point with their lips," he said, pointing his lips into the air like he was trying to kiss something he couldn't reach. "Most Chileans will deny this, but it is a natural thing that everyone does without thinking."

The more I learnt, it seemed, the more relaxed became my attitude about Chile and its people. Sometimes clichés were true. Education and understanding were the most effective ways to break down cultural barriers. There really wasn't that much of a difference between our two peoples. Yes, every aspect of the culture, language, customs, and beliefs was different, but at the core of it all we had the same fears, and the same joys. We all wanted to do well in life, to enjoy time spent with those we cared about, and to have something that drove us. For me, it was the ocean and surfing, but for Rodrigo, it was family, yet we both sat here, side-by-side, enjoying each other's company like old mates.

For the remainder of the bus ride, I didn't say much and listened to Rodrigo. It was nice and I felt at peace, his words gentle and calm, light but educated. After a while, I wasn't focused on what he was saying, but rather enjoying his voice as it faded into the background. For the first time, I became curious about my family, who they were, and what they would be like. Rodrigo was mid-sentence about the towns surrounding Concepcion and how on one side in the town of Tome, you could buy fresh crab on the street for a dollar, when suddenly he stood up to look around. "This is our stop. *Oye senor, pare por aqui por favor!*"

Sneaking a look out the window as the bus began to slow, I was surprised to see nothing that resembled a city, rather the muddy outskirts of a town. Noticing my confused expression, Rodrigo turned to me. "We are still about 30 minutes from Concepcion, that's why it looks so barren. We have to get off here, but I will take you to 'Conce' another day so that you can see how magnificent it is."

Somehow, Rodrigo always seemed to have a way with words and I wondered if he was a father himself. If not, he should adopt some kids and speak to them just like that. After we retrieved our luggage, the bus drove off, leaving us on the side of the road. It made me think of a movie where the spy waited by a station for a message to be delivered or a villain to pick him up and I half expected a Russian guy in a black BMW to drive up and say to us through a half-cracked window, "Get in zee car if you want to live."

"How long until the next bus?" I asked Rodrigo.

"Err, about an hour. There is a lady selling empanadas across the street. Are you hungry?"

"Starving," I said, suddenly ravenous and realising I hadn't eaten since I was on the plane. A little lady, no more than five feet tall sat next to a portable oven at the bus stop across the street. It seemed strange, almost out of place, but the street food was the best place to experience local cuisine. This would be a great opportunity to practise my Spanish, and if I was confident enough and stuck to the basics, I reckon I could get away with pretending to be a Chilean.

"*Que Querii amorcito?*"

Bam. Smacked in the face with words I had never heard in my life, spoken so fast that it all seemed to expel from her lips in one breath. Dumbfounded, all previous confidence out the window. So much for knowing Spanish

"*Dos empanaditas de pollo*," responded Rodrigo, shooting me a wink and trying to conceal the smile creeping up on his face. It was as if he knew a secret, gaining great satisfaction from watching my struggle. I would come to learn that this was a common fact among the Chilean people, their dialect spoken much like the country folk of Australia spoke English. It was such a variant of Spanish, only they could understand it and many outsiders couldn't. Chileans knew this and were very proud of it, not taking the opportunity to slow down for a non-Chilean but relishing the unique struggle they got to observe as someone tried to communicate. In a paradoxical fashion, the Chileans were extremely helpful, but when it came to language, you were on your own.

On receiving our steaming, savoury pastries, we made our way back across the street to find refuge on a bench under cover. Taking our seats, I enthusiastically bit into the empanada, causing hot cheese to explode into my mouth, burning my tongue. Rodrigo passed me some water and seeing that my mouth had recovered asked me why I was here.

A little perplexed by what I thought was an obvious answer, I asked for further clarification, my chest tightening as fear of an unknown, potentially personal question brought about a cloud of discomfort. This wasn't because I thought Rodrigo was being intrusive, but because I was afraid of revealing something I didn't want others to know.

"You have never visited, nor have you ever met your family. Yet, out of nowhere you are just here. I am just curious as to why now? Why not when your father died or any other time that we wanted to be a part of your life? We haven't heard anything about you since his passing."

I started to shake. The deepest question I never expected to get, and I definitely wasn't ready to answer. In an effort to save face, I took a deep breath and looked away so Rodrigo couldn't see the water accumulating in my eyes. "Why does it matter? Do you not want me here? I can just leave if you don't." Rodrigo didn't deserve to be treated like this. Feeling so vulnerable, I reacted the only way I knew how. Was it too much to ask to just enjoy the trip?

"I'm sorry. I didn't mean to upset you," Rodrigo said softly, realising that he had been too direct too early. Not wanting to upset me further and potentially lose the chance for me to connect with my family, he changed his tone completely. "I hope you do stay."

The rest of the wait went by in silence. I could feel Rodrigo next to me but refused to look at him, instead observing the empanada lady across the street, watching as she continued to serve other customers, slowly selling all of the empanadas she had made. It would be a good day for her and I wondered if every day was so successful, having a constant stream of clients drawn by the delicious aromas empanadas emit during long waits for the bus. Certainly she had a reputation, building a customer base from the regular locals who used the stop. Life seemed so simple for her and it made me wonder if my life would ever return to a daily repetition of the things that I enjoyed.

The bus arrived and we boarded in silence. Sitting next to Rodrigo again reminded me of the kindness he had shown to a complete stranger in Chillan, embracing me as an old friend through a one-sided connection born out the friendship with my father. "I'm sorry Rodrigo. I shouldn't have yelled at you."

"It's okay. How do you say? No worries." Rodrigo replied smiling. "I have a lot of questions, as I'm sure everyone will. Maybe I was a little full on, too soon."

"I get it. I'm just not ready to answer those questions yet. I need time."

We arrived in Copquecura within an hour, driving over the crest of a hill to the sight of a spectacular panorama as we entered the city from the east. The entire Pacific Ocean stretched out in front of me, cuddled by a small town expanding from its beach eastward into the hill from which I approached.

My grandma's house was where I'd be staying. It was only a few blocks from the bus station and Rodrigo suggested that we walk. Although a white cement house like every other, it was very obvious that we had arrived at the correct one. Displayed across the entire front porch was a four-metre-wide banner saying "*Bienvenido* Mari!" And the smell of sausages being barbequed greeted us, a good indication that this would not be a relaxing and quiet afternoon.

"*Alo!*" yelled Rodrigo through the fence.

A few minutes later, a short, old, slightly round lady opened the door. We made eye contact for only a moment before all pandemonium broke loose. She suddenly turned and yelled something behind her before hobbling down the driveway faster than I had ever seen anyone 'hobble'. I couldn't help but smile at the scene in front of me, trying my hardest to refrain from bursting into a fit of laughter.

"*Dios mio! Mi preciosa hija! Como estas? No lo puedo creer!* You're finally here, my granddaughter is here!"

She seemed elated to see me and embraced me so tightly I had to really concentrate so as to not pass out, feeling like a fish who had just been befriended by a child, squirming to get back into the water. Following the near-death experience, I was ushered into the house, Rodrigo joyfully following close behind, hoping to capture more of the spectacle. In a blur I was taken through the front hallway, my bags stripped from me as I was shoved through a heavy door into the backyard. As my eyes adjusted to the light, I could see at least ten people gathered around a charcoal barbeque, all with a drink in hand and cheerfully chatting, only to stop and stare at the bewildered newcomer.

"*Les presento a mi nieta*, Mari," my grandma said, following close behind to ensure everyone knew I was hers.

Stunned, I was not sure what to do. Luckily, this was not a problem in Chile as one by one, every single guest came up to me and kissed me on the cheek, saying something along the lines of "It is great to finally meet you."

Being an Australian, this was all still extremely unfamiliar to me. With a laid-back Aussie attitude, easy going and ready to have a chat with everyone, especially if it was about surf, I was taken aback by the formality of interacting with others. Somehow more intimate, complete strangers treated me like a close relative. Elsewhere in the world, Australians were known as being the open and friendly people. But experiencing this Chilean form of immediate acceptance, I think we have seriously missed something.

"Would you like a beer?" said Rodrigo, trying to distract me from the onslaught. "There are some really good ones that were picked up from the shop. I recommend a Kuntsmann."

"I don't drink beer thank you, just a glass of water please." I did want a beer, but I had made a promise to Boedi, and I wasn't going to break it on the first day. As Rodrigo left to fetch me a glass of water, I tried to participate in the party as best as I could. This was made easier by my grandma, who seemed glued to my hip and had made it her mission to ensure everyone knew who I was. Out of nowhere she started telling everyone all about me, including some details I didn't think anyone would know. She spoke of my surfing, my odd habits, my childhood stories, basically anything good from my life that came to mind. "How do you know all of this stuff?" I whispered in her ear. "Your father wrote to me about you," she replied. "He was so proud of you."

Fuck. Time to hold back tears again.

A couple hours later, the guests started to go home, leaving the house quiet for the first time since my arrival. Offering to help clean up, I was told instead that I should go and rest. I couldn't agree more and finding the most comfortable-looking couch, I lied down, not moving again for ten hours.

Waking up to a completely still house, the sun was just beginning to stir. It must have been early, maybe five o'clock. As I entered the kitchen to grab a glass of water a view of the ocean greeted me through the window above the sink, its small breeze driven waves lightly slapping the black sands as it woke up the earth around it.

Becalmed by the tranquillity which had welcomed me to the day, my gaze seemed fixed to the sea, where I noticed a strong northbound current and took note of its consistent movement. Remembering that Rodrigo had told me about a great surf spot that lied off a point just outside town, it seemed like the perfect opportunity to explore and without hesitation, I borrowed the bicycle from the back of the house and headed north.

The waves here were amazing. A big southerly swell caught the point perfectly, wrapping itself into peeling seven-foot barrels. There was a rocky shoreline and I could see the swell getting trapped into the pocket with only one way to exit, creating a strong sweep out away from the point. It reminded me of my home beach: Alex Heads. Waiting at the top of the hill I watched the water move, appreciative of its beauty, hoping to understand the waves before going in. It was a practice instilled in me by my surf mentors to respect the ocean, it prepared me to make the right decisions on what to expect, which board to take, where to enter and exit the water and of course, how to best surf the waves.

For such a small, middle of nowhere town, I was surprised at the number of surfers in the water. There had to be twenty at least, sitting on their boards in the angled line that you see in every session, waiting for their turn to ride the wave of their life. I could see the easiest way to enter was right at the end of the point, jumping off the rocks onto a wave and paddling out of the way of the boulders before the other waves arrived and washed you ashore. From there, a gentle back eddy would give me enough of a break in the waves to paddle out without too much difficulty, having to only duck dive the bigger waves. As I made my way down to the water's edge, I saw a guy stretching on the sand, getting ready to go out as well.

"Hey, Esperame!" I yelled out, hoping to paddle out with a local. He turned around and nodded in agreement to paddle together, giving me a fist bump as I approached him. "Cheers mate. I'm Mari," I greeted him as I quickly stretched.

"Ahh a gringa. I'm Boris," he replied, happy to have made a new friend.

We walked the rocks together and arrived at the jump point I had seen earlier. It turned out I was correct, and Boris certified that this would be the best spot to enter. He jumped in first, paddling hard to avoid the oncoming wave. Following his lead, I entered close behind to join him, paddling in unison through the oncoming whitewash and duck diving when necessary, but trying to navigate through the breaks to avoid becoming fatigued or getting stuck.

It was a longer paddle than I expected and after five minutes, we finally arrived at the line-up. The sets were coming in consistently and were well spaced apart, providing me with ample time to talk to my new friend without having to worry about constantly watching out for unexpected waves.

Boris knew enough English to get his point across as we tried to maintain a basic conversation. It turned out he learnt English from an old friend of his, another Australian whom he had met while living in Chile as a university student. They had spent so much time together: Surfing, partying, and studying, that he was able to pick up some of the lingo. Boris lived in the town of Quirique, but his family owned a cabin close by, allowing him the opportunity to spend every summer surfing at every opportunity, catching rides to the beach by hitchhiking, horse riding or in the worst case, walking.

The next set arrived and we were in the best spot to catch the first two waves. Knowing the first wave was generally the worst, I tried to let Boris have it. It didn't work, as Boris knew exactly what I was trying to do and missed the wave on purpose to have a chance at a better one. "I live on these waves. You can't fool me!" he laughed. "It is okay, we can catch the next one together, I don't mind."

As the next wave approached, we paddled hard, keeping a distance between us to ensure we didn't collide. A great idea at first, but it didn't work as I was too far forward on the wave and unable to generate enough speed. Boris was too deep and as I dragged my hand along the water to regress back into the wave, I saw Boris get knocked off and crash into the white wash. Sinking into the pocket, I bent down further to improve my balance and gain more speed. The wave dissipated and I shot over to the back side of the wave. Paddling back, I watched as other surfers took the remaining waves, dodging Boris as he made his way through the onslaught of dumping water, and back to the line-up. It was a monstrous effort, fighting the sweep which persistently pushed me away from the break point. Quickly becoming exhausted, I saw Boris catch another wave, this time he was well positioned and able to pull off three consecutive turns and tucks. He passed behind me and I stopped paddling, raised my fist and yelled out in support. "YEEEEWWWWWWW!" I screamed at the top of my lungs.

With one final bottom turn, he flew over the top of the wave like superman and landed in the calm water on the other side. It was a well-executed ride, and I was instantly inspired to end the session with a wave just as good. Another hour went by and I was unable to catch a wave, constantly having to give right of way to the other surfers. I started to shake as the freezing waters of the Humboldt Current that came up from Antarctica pierced right through my wetsuit. Like most surfers, I refused to go in without catching a wave all the way to shore.

Soon enough, a new set approached from the horizon and reading its direction, I believed I was in the perfect position to catch a wave. My prediction was correct and as the third wave of the set came in, I paddled hard and popped up. It was straighter than I first believed, closing out as I reached the bottom of the wave, indicating that it was time to go in and ending my first Chilean surf session.

As I popped down onto my stomach and rode the white-water into the black-sand beach, it seemed that Boris had decided to wait for me and clapped as I approached the shore. Held out of the water by my board, I warmed up rapidly as the sun heated the black rubber wetsuit that covered me. Reaching the beach, I picked up my board and walked up to meet Boris, who was now sitting on the bench next to the road. "Bloody awesome sesh," I said enthusiastically. "We should surf again together while I'm here."

"Yes gringa, I think that is a good idea," he responded, smiling.

We exchanged details and I walked back to my grandma's bicycle, happy to have made a surf mate in Chile. The ride back to Copquecura went quickly and I entered the house in a surprisingly good mood. I could smell rich flavours of a fish dinner, wafting from the kitchen and engulfing the entire house. An unfamiliar smell of a meal I have never tasted, I was brought back to reality and reminded once again that I was in another country. "Wow that smells amazing," I proclaimed as I entered the kitchen. "What's for lunch?"

"Sopa de Mariscos," my grandma responded. "It will stop you from getting sick."

"I'm not going to get sick. Why do you think that?" I asked in response to the seemingly peculiar premonition.

"Because you have been in the cold water. Now go take a hot shower, and don't take too long, the soup is almost ready."

Chileans were quite superstitious, but I did as I was told. It was certainly not worth a fight, and a shower did sound appealing. I walked back into the kitchen feeling as refreshed as ever and was greeted by a feast. On the table lied a red tablecloth laden with an assortment of breads and cheeses, a bottle of wine, and other finger delicacies, all surrounding the main course, Sopa de Mariscos.

Sitting down, I helped myself to everything, stuffing my face full of all the dishes within reach. So involved in eating the food in front of me, I was not paying attention to my surroundings and was unaware of how rude I must have looked. Patiently, my grandma sat in silence, drinking her tea and helping herself to some bread. She watched me, observing, purposefully ignoring my behaviour, but intently examining my character, trying to figure out if I truly was the daughter of her son. Twenty minutes went by in silence as I continued to stuff my face. Getting very full, I leaned back in my chair and stretched my arms. Tired and full, I could probably have gone for another nap. Suddenly, I was hit in the face by a piece of bread. "Lower your arms! Don't be so rude," scolded my grandma sternly, having thrown her bread intentionally trying to teach me a lesson.

"Whaa? I didn't know that was rude. Pardon me. The food is delicious by the way. Thank you."

She smiled in response and stood up, collecting the empty bowls and beginning to clear the table. Staying seated to finish my tea, my gaze once again turned to the ocean. I just watched it, mesmerised, not so much lost in thought as lost in feeling. An inexplicable attraction, it was something I couldn't control, losing myself to its depths, letting it take me as far as the ocean was wide.

"You know, your father used to do the same thing," my grandma said, distracting me from my solace and continuing to observe me from the kitchen. "He would just sit there for hours, watching the waves. I don't get it. It's just the same ocean as every other day."

Not wanting to attempt to explain the comfort it provided without sounding crazy, I recounted how dad and I used to watch the ocean all the time. How we would often get a coffee at the local café after surfing or even on a calm day and just sit there, observing and enjoying how the water moved. It was like reading a book, except this one you could read together. We'd talk too, about everything and anything. I'd tell him about my day, anything that went wrong, things I wanted to do, boys I liked. But beyond it all, we'd talk about the surf. I really wanted to sail around the world, surfing and living on the water. We discussed it a lot, but my dad did not want anything to do with it. I couldn't understand why someone who loved the ocean so much would not want to get a boat. It didn't make sense. He used to own a boat too.

"It sounds like you were very close to him," suggested my grandma, staring at me now, not in an analytical way, but sympathetically. "But there is still a lot you don't understand."

"Hey, listen. I knew my dad better than anyone. He and I were very close. Don't come at me with that shit!" I yelled, grievously offended at the idea that my father could be anything less than the immortalised image of how I remembered him.

"Don't you dare talk to me like that. I am your grandma. Show some respect."

"Earn it then!" I stormed out of the room, fury and sadness coursing through my veins. I couldn't sit still. I needed a way to relax. To switch off. Storming into my room, I grabbed my surfboard before running as fast as I could through the back garden and down toward the cool black sand beach.

As hard and fast as possible, I paddled out to sea. Stroke after stroke, I could feel my arms burning, my breathing heavy as I pushed through the water, gliding along the surface like a plane through the sky. After about an hour I stopped, exhausted. I lied there on my stomach, catching my breath. My eyes were closed and I felt the motion of the water as I bobbed up and down like a cork.

It was impossible to know how long I stayed like that. I may have even fallen asleep. So calm, more comfortable here by myself, with just my thoughts and surrounded by the thing I loved the most. A light splashing sounded from behind me. It must have been fish or maybe some white water and whether the sound was actually real or just a dream, either way I was too comfortable to check or care for that matter.

The sound became more distinct, and it appeared to be getting closer. I sat up slowly, my eyes fluttering open as I turned to see what was making the noise when I was greeted by a familiar face. "Hey!" said Rodrigo, bumping his longboard into mine. "That's a long paddle. You must be in great shape."

I looked around. I couldn't see land anywhere. "Fuck, we must be five kilometres from shore. Why did you paddle all the way out here?"

"It sure feels like it," panted Rodrigo, still trying to catch his breath. "You've been gone for six hours and I've been looking for you for at least two. I stopped by your grandma's house to see if you wanted to come for a drive up the coast, and she told me that you got angry and stormed out. Are you okay?"

"Yeah I'm okay now. I just got a bit upset and needed to clear my head. I didn't mean to offend her. I'm a bit testier as of late."

"What is going on with you? You seem like a kind person, but since we have met, this is the second outburst you have had."

"Aww nah, I'm okay. I think I'm just going through withdrawals. I drank a lot before I came here, and I promised my mate I wouldn't drink while I was in Chile."

I was telling the truth. Without the numbing effects of alcohol, I have had to confront the reality of my faults, my emotions, and my past. My consumption of alcohol was a problem, but it wasn't the root cause of what I was going through. How could I explain that to someone I have just met? Sure, he seemed very trustworthy as a person and I felt like I have known him my entire life, but I wasn't not a bitch. I wasn't going to spill my beans to a complete stranger. I couldn't even articulate the problem, unable to face it myself and come to terms with the catalyst of my internal sadness. If I couldn't do it for me, how could I do it for another?

Obviously, Rodrigo didn't believe me, and could see right through my shitty response. However, he didn't call my bluff, as he had too much class for that. He had the emotional intelligence of the bloody Dalai Llama. "Okay, I understand," Rodrigo said. "But maybe it will help you to embrace those around you rather than push them away. I am here to help if you need it. If you don't, I am here anyway." "Cheers. I think I can tackle it on my own, but I appreciate the offer."

"Any time," replied Rodrigo. "The onshore wind is picking up, we should start paddling back, fast."

Soon enough, I understood what he meant. The wind came out of nowhere, blowing in from out at sea and intensifying with every minute. We paddled hard, long consistent powerful strokes, deep purposeful breaths. The wind was to our backs, but it didn't mean shit. With the waves increasing and the current against us, the water slowly became a washing machine. It was slow going and our situation quickly got out of hand. This wasn't Australia. No one was coming to save you.

"We should tie together!" yelled Rodrigo over the wind. "That way we don't lose each other!"

We stopped paddling and untied the cordolette which attached the leg rope to my board. As per Rodrigo's instructions, I weaved my leg rope through the cordolette. Rodrigo had done the same, and we tied the two ends together. It was weird, but by far the best way to attach ourselves to each other and still be attached to our boards. This method made us safer, but it made it harder to paddle and we had to maintain a solid rhythm to make it work. It seemed pretty straightforward in theory, but with the waves gaining in size, it was no walk in the park.

For two and a half hours we paddled harder than I have ever paddled in my life. Rodrigo had not even had a rest from his paddle out to me and it was beginning to show. He was trying his best, staring out in front with an unrelenting determination, however, soon enough he began to lose pace. "We must still be about three k's from shore, I can see the lights," I yelled without stopping. "Let me take the lead."

I switched onto his longboard. Being larger and faster, it would be better for carrying the load. Rodrigo hopped on my board, sitting further back to allow the lip to rise out of the water. Slowly, like a train heading uphill, we paddled. It seemed to work. Using my remaining strength to set the pace, Rodrigo was now following in my wake, keeping up so as to take some of the strain off me.

An hour later we collapsed on the beach, wet and exhausted. It took everything we had to walk back to my grandma's house, and we finally crashed through the door in a state of delirious exhaustion. I didn't even bother taking a hot shower, but dried off quickly before falling asleep under a mountain of blankets, unmoved for the following twelve hours.

Over the next week it was impossible to go surfing. The winds that came during my last paddle hadn't stopped and the water had become a mad washing machine. It wasn't even worth trying to get wet and I was forced to get to know the town. This meant accompanying my grandma to the markets, going to neighbourhood barbeques, and having a lot of spare nights to read.

My grandma had chosen to either forget or forgive my outburst. Either way, we seemed to be getting along well. Talking about everything and anything that came to mind, we began to bond. Slowly, I felt as if I was actually part of the family. It seemed that I had met everyone in town, yet I was still to meet anyone else in my actual family. Now that I thought about it, I didn't even know if I had any additional family. I had always assumed because my dad was Chilean, his must be huge, but I'd never really bothered to ask. On the eighth day following the paddle with Rodrigo, I arrived home after another Chilean barbeque. Exhausted and full to the brim with Chilean sausages or 'Longaniza', I quickly found my way to bed and was asleep before my head even hit the pillow.

Suddenly surrounded by water, I looked around and realised I was at the bottom of the ocean again. Everything was so brilliant, every colour vibrant, every feature alive. I watched as multi-patterned and different sized fish swam past, going about their day without any awareness of me floating next to them. It was completely surreal and I could only imagine what it would be like to really be here. Above me, I could see the waves crashing on the surface. The intensity of Mother Nature without the noise was always incredibly beautiful and I watched the wave perform in a series of acrobatic moves you would expect to see at Cirque Du Solei. The admiration lasted mere seconds, as I could feel the pressure rapidly building in my chest. The urge to breathe became very apparent and without any hesitation I attempted to take a breath. Big mistake. My mouth flooded with water and with great difficulty I managed to cough it up before it entered my lungs.

I couldn't hear anything but I could feel everything. My chest was hurting and I was fighting the urge to breathe. I tried to scream out, but was greeted with only bubbles, comically innocent as they floated away towards salvation. I realised I was panicking and, in an attempt to keep my heart rate low, I tried desperately to maintain my focus. It all felt so real. But it couldn't be.

The struggle continued, somehow stuck, with no idea as to why. Writhing, I tried unsuccessfully to swim towards the surface, somehow hoping that if I willed it hard enough, I may be able to break the water and take a massive gulp of air. Nothing was working, and I refused to give up, continuing to stare at the surface as it began to fade away, slowly overtaken by darkness as I drifted out of consciousness...

I woke up in a fit of coughing, unable to breathe and rolled over the side of the bed in an effort to vomit, dry heaving as I tried to catch my breath. Sweating, my eyes watering and throat burning as I fought to stop the uncontrollable shaking. I could have sworn I wasn't dreaming. Unable to relax from the confusion and trauma of my dream, I made my way into the bathroom to wash my face and clean my mouth out. Observing my reflection in the mirror, I saw my eyes laced with deep red veins, my skin was pale, and I looked physically exhausted. I stood there for five minutes breathing to calm down, repeatedly washing my face. Soon enough, the colour returned to my face and I started to feel better. As the redness faded from my eyes, so did the memory of the dream.

"*Estas bien?*" my grandma called out from the bedroom door. "You sound sick."

"Yeah, I'm all right, I just choked on some water."

Coming into the kitchen to make some breakfast, I was surprised to see boxes all over the counters and questioned my grandma as I navigated my way around them to the table. She moved a box, giving me space to sit down and served me some buttered toast, before telling me that she had something that she wanted to show me. For some reason, I didn't think she'd go to all of this effort for good news and I could feel a pressure building in my chest.

"We both know your father from opposite sides of his life," she began. "The first time I heard from him after he left Chile, he had sent me a letter. More of a memoir, it was his way of telling me that everything was okay, and to let me know what had happened to him. This is the link between us. I want you to know your father's story."

Feeling myself begin to hyperventilate, I stared at my grandma as she handed me the memoir. "I don't know if I can do this," I stammered, my eyes starting to water.

"I believe in you," she said with confidence. "I think this will help you let go. I'll be right here with you." She sat down, wrapping her arms around me as I unfolded the story of how my father came to Australia...

Breathe.

Chapter 6

I left Chile in such a rush that I never had the chance to say good bye. The emotions experienced in recent days had left me ill equipped to cope with what lay ahead. Saying goodbye to the old man and motoring out of the bay, the gravity of my journey set in; I had never sailed. I didn't know where I would end up, and I was still in Chilean waters.

With relative ease, the first days passed, a gentle breeze consistently blowing without much change from its south-easterly direction, which gave me ample time to practise all of the skills and systems the old man had taught me. The theory was one thing, but I found the practice quite difficult.

After motoring all night to get clear of the coastline, I cut the engine, the boat gently slowing down. Following the old man's direction, I unfurled the main sail successfully, tying the rigging lines and setting course for Rapanui. The sail caught the wind, pulling the boat with ease on a slight starboard lean as I drifted through the water, slicing the waves like a knife through butter.

I hauled in the main sail, then unfurled it again checking to make sure I was doing it correctly. Tacking and jibing, using the genoa and trying to read the winds to predict oncoming weather, it was so much fun that I momentarily forgot everything that had been going on. For one brief instance, I was at peace, alone on the water, exhilarated by this newfound passion and way of seeing the world.

Having not slept in days and spending all day running about the boat, I was exhausted by six o'clock. With the sun setting, I lay down in my hammock, gently swinging from the mast as the sun descended in a spirit of golden orange. Before I knew it I had fallen asleep.

"What are you going to do? Make me disappear? Do it, I dare you, but I swear, when I get out, I will hunt you down, and I will end you!" *BANG!*

Panting and shaking uncontrollably, I sat up before losing my balance and falling out of the hammock to collapse on the deck, only to rock back and forth as I relived my brother's murder. There he was, forced into the dirt, knees bleeding as they dug into the rocks yet unnoticed as he stared into the face of his killer, anger and courage pouring from my brother's eyes, only to be shot, the anger fading with the life inside him. With everything going on, the memory of his demise had been pushed back to the depths of my subconscious, imprinting itself in my memory, only to resurface easily as I let my defences down during sleep.

Slowly I regained my composure. The shock of the nightmare faded as I came back to reality. Sitting there, I stared out into the darkness, all of my senses heightened. Feeling the cool breeze against my back, I could smell the salt rising from the water, could hear the waves splashing against the side of the boat, yet all I could see was darkness. For the first time, I felt completely alone.

Sleep didn't come back to me, and I remained immobile for the rest of the night, my mind wandering to every possibility as my body bobbed like a cork in natural rhythm with the ocean current. As the night broke, so did my anguish, the sunrise giving light to a new day and bringing with it peace. Without the backdrop of darkness, the images of my brother's death faded, allowing me to move on and continue my journey, even if just for the time being.

The following days and weeks were much the same: A constant oscillation of bliss and agony, a sick form of entertainment for the ocean gods. Every morning waking up to a paradise. Every night fearing the oncoming hell. It haunted me like a ghost, driving me crazy, the only solace the constant movement of the water, rocking me to sleep late at night like a mother caring for her child.

After a month at sea I was desperate to get off the boat, to have someone to speak with and to start life anew. I didn't know the date, but I did know it was a Wednesday. It was that morning I woke up to the most beautiful site in the world, Rapa Nui.

Rapa Nui or I think it was called it Easter Island now was the most isolated island in the world. Further away from any other land on earth, it was surrounded by high cliffs, the coastline scattered with statues called 'Moai' that protected the island and the people who inhabited it. So beautiful, it was here that I thought I had finally found refuge.

"*Hola, esto es la Navy de Chile, identifíquete,*" sounded a voice over the radio.

My heart stopped. The Chilean navy was here. They must control the island. Fuck! If they found me, they would connect me to my brother and imprison me or worse.

"*Hola, esto es la Navy de Chile, identifíquete,*" came the voice again.

Thinking quickly, I searched the entire boat for anything that could help me out. Hastily diving through the port side cupboard, I noticed a French flag lying on the ground. It was my only shot. Carrying the flag back up on deck, I flung it over the mast.

"*Hola, esto es la Navy de Chile, identifíquete!*" the same voice screamed.

Taking a deep breath, I thought as hard as I could back to the French classes I took in school and with desperate confidence, I responded using the best French accent I could, hoping that like most Chileans, they won't know what a real French accent sounds like. "Err, bonjour. Hello, my name is Francis, do you speak English or French?"

"Identify yourself," said the man on the radio, this time in English.

"Err, my name is Francis, I am from France, I am sailing to Tahiti," I improvised. I reckon in a different situation, I could have been a good actor. There was a long pause. Unsure what was going on, I held my breath, waiting for anything other than being boarded or bombed.

"This is Chilean territory, you are trespassing, leave our waters now or you will be shot!" screamed the voice.

"Err, I am leaving now, good day." Confused, but not willing to wait around, I immediately turned on the motor and redirected the boat southeast, travelling as fast as I could away from the island. Why hadn't they boarded? Why didn't they just shoot or arrest me? It wasn't until many years later that I discovered the French were playing both sides of the fence: Accepting political refugees, but at the same time secretly collaborating with Pinochet. France's inability to choose one side over the other had saved my life.

At fast as I could, I continued west. With barely any wind, I used the motor the entire time, stupidly as I wasn't being chased. For two days, my fears of getting caught along with trying to avoid my nightly torture kept me awake. I pushed through the nights, bow pointed towards the setting sun. Not eating, not dreaming, wasting away into a fit of sleep deprived hallucinations until finally on the eve of the third day, I collapsed on the deck.

Feeling like I had been hit by a truck, I finally awoke to the sun rising above me. My energy renewed and my mind becalmed, I was reborn with an unfamiliar peace. How long I was asleep, I don't know, but my body had received the rest I needed to continue on my journey.

Tying a rope to my leg for safety, I jumped into the ocean. From the moment I touched the water, I could feel the salt water wash over me like a bath, its coolness rehydrating as I swam around to appreciate my surroundings. It's inexplicable that feeling, cleansing the body and mind in a way which can only be described in biblical terms.

The next few days I found to be some of the best of my life. So occupied with my daily tasks, night fell quickly, darkness blanketing the earth, accompanied by a drowsiness that arrived with the fading light. I fell asleep with ease, with only a few brief moments of anguish brought about by a bad dream.

As long as the waves weren't too big, my days always started with a leap into the ocean. I dried myself off, ate a breakfast of porridge accompanied by a cup of tea, and began my daily routine. This began by checking my location and marking it on a map to track my progress across the Pacific and make sure I didn't drift in the wrong direction. Too far north, and I would enter the doldrums: A place cursed with no winds. If I travel too far south, I would be fighting against a current and would struggle to stay on course. It was essential to stay in the sweet spot. My inadequate sailing experience depended on it.

After I worked out my location, I measured the wind and set my course for the day before casting the fishing lines out the back of the boat to catch as much food as possible while as I sailed. Having been denied a stopover in Rapa Nui, my supplies had to go further, so catching a fish would determine if I ate dinner.

The days carried on in the same cycle whilst constantly readjusting the sails and rigging in accordance with the wind. With each day the process got easier, my skills becoming increasingly fine-tuned as I tried to maximise my speed and efficiency in the water. It was the beginning of a love for sailing and found that no longer was solitude my prison, but rather my liberator. I sang naked from the bow, drew pictures of my surroundings, and even tied myself to the boat to be dragged behind through the water.

During my third week since passing Rapa Nui, I woke up to a heavy rain pounding the deck. Enjoying the first rain of the trip, I didn't think much of it, and continued my day as usual, with the added bonus of getting to wear a poncho and drink lots of tea. By noon, things had taken a turn for the worst. The swell picked up tremendously and the boat began to rise and fall, smashing the bow into the sea as water continually surged over the deck only to spill back into the ocean on the other side. The wind howled with such a force it would challenge wolves to hide in their caves. The main sail was still up, catching the winds and causing the boat to be flung around like a rag doll. Desperate, I tried to remember what the old man had said as I was thrown from side to side, unbalanced in the boat from hell.

"A reeve!" I yelled. "I have to take a reeve. Wait, what the fuck is a reeve?" Not able to remember, I had no other choice but to take the sail down to save the boat and my life. The rain shot me with a tremendous sting as if it were made of needles, pelting down from every direction. Drenched to the bone and freezing, I grabbed at the line to loosen the sail enough to pull it down. Without warning, I watched in horror as the sail ripped straight down the centre, flapping in two pieces and continuing to shred as the wind took to it with gusto. My heart sank. There was nothing I could do. I lowered the sail and packed it up as best I could in its current broken state, not knowing if I would ever be able to fix it.

With no other option but to wait out the storm knowing it had already achieved its first victory I crawled into my bed and lay down staring at the ceiling. Frightened for my life, I feared that at any moment a wave would come and wash me away. It never did.

Slowly, the winds calmed and the seas quietened. The boat sat in the water, drifting defeated through an innocent looking sea, broken and in ruin. With no more engine fuel, no mast, and no resupply in Rapa Nui, I suddenly realised the magnitude of my predicament. With no way to navigate I was at the complete mercy of the ocean. To where it would take me I did not know, nor did I have time to find out. First a fugitive then a castaway, alone in the Pacific with no hope of finding my way. I could only hope to be picked up by a passing boat or that I found land, quickly.

For the next three weeks I watched as my body washed away like the ebbing tide. Having to ration my food, I was down to half a cup of lentils and a piece of cheese a day. Fishing was hopeless. I cast a hundred times, a thousand, nothing. The only thing within my control was my mind. With the attitude of a Chilean bull, I refused to give up. I left Chile for a reason. To live another day. To give myself and my family a fighting chance for a future. If I gave up, I would disgrace my family, myself, and most importantly my brother.

One month turned into two. Now out of food, I was desperate. With little energy I lay on the deck, taking in the warmth of the sun while reciting out loud the recipes of Chilean dishes my mother once cooked for me. Lentejas, Sopa de Mariscos, Torta Aleman, Empanadas de Pollo, etc. As I imagined myself sitting at the table on a Sunday afternoon, I could taste the flavours in my mouth, brother by my side, toasting a glass of Malbec wine to a day of quintessential bliss only found in the fond memories of the ones you love.

Was I delusional? Was I dead already? Was I clinging onto the only thing that was keeping me alive? I was adrift both literally and in the depths of my soul, clinging to life through thought and memory alone, feeling nothing and everything at once. It was ironic how shit my situation was, yet I had not shit in two weeks. One morning I woke up in the same mindless routine and sat up to go up on deck.

"Ow!" I yelled in pain, having hit my head on a large metal object. I opened my eyes. Above me lay another bed. I was on the lower bed of a metal-framed bunk bed attached to the wall. Ducking to stand out of bed, I felt a sudden prick in my arm. I looked down to see an IV sticking into it.

"Hello?"

All of a sudden, a middle-aged blonde woman in a nurse's uniform entered the room. Worried that I was standing, she immediately asked me to sit down, saying I needed to rest.

"Where am I? How did I get here?" I asked, sitting down on the bed as I was told.

"This is the HMAS Derwent," she informed me. "You were found adrift, so we brought you aboard. You were in really bad shape and we thought we had lost you for a while. Please hold your arm still."

I watched as she pulled the IV out of my arm, careful to apply pressure to the lesion to prevent it from bleeding. "Thank you. You saved my life. Literally."

She smiled as she stood back up. Turning to leave the room, she stopped at the door. "Welcome to the Cook Islands," she said before disappearing from view.

I came to learn I had drifted further north than I originally thought, almost literally running into the Royal Australian Navy a few hundred kilometres off the coast of the Cook Islands, a territory of Australia. For three weeks I stayed on the ship, slowly regaining my strength, and discovering the horror of the situation in my home country. Torture, state-controlled media, a complete takeover of all institutions and curfews put into place. All those who publicly opposed the regime or had supported the previous government were 'missing'.

Of course, this news was coming from a country that did not support the new government of Chile, so I was cautious to take their words with a grain of salt. However, I had also seen first-hand what the government of Chile had done to my family, and I feared the worst for my compatriots.

If I returned to my homeland I would be killed and I imagined the worst as the Royal Australian Ship sailed back to the port of Brisbane. To make matters worse, I was informed that the moment we docked, I was to be escorted to the Department of Immigration so they could work out what to do with me.

To take my mind off my unforeseen future, I spent my days helping out on the ship, and the evenings playing cards in the mess hall. It was easy to get to know people, all of whom were happy to see a new face after months at sea and equally I was pleased to call them my friends, even if just for the moment. They would never know and I will never tell them, but they did so much more for me than I could ever express. They saved my life.

Arriving in Brisbane, I was greeted by two smartly dressed officers who were to escort me to my fate. We drove in silence as I sat in the back, patiently trying not to think of what was to become of me, instead taking in my new surroundings. So different from Chile: The houses were bigger, the cars drove on the opposite side of the road, and nearly all the people were white, the majority of whom were walking around in sandals. In the ten minutes since my arrival I was in awe of the world around me.

Following a 30-minute drive to the immigration office and another three hours waiting to be attended to, I was finally called into the Office of Foreign Affairs. A small gentleman in a black suit motioned me to sit down at his desk, asking me if I would like a cup of tea.

"No, thank you. I really just want to know what is to become of me."

Taking a sip of his tea, the small man in the suit sat up in his chair, straightening himself and trying to gain a few inches in height in order to assert some sort of authority. "The captain has informed us of your situation. Based on the danger imposed on your person should we send you home, and the lack of support the Australian government has for Chile during this time, we have agreed to grant you political asylum. If you choose, you may stay in Australia indefinitely. Although to make it official, you will need to sign some paperwork of course."

I began to cry. Wiping tears from my face, I stood up, shaking the poor man's hand so hard I was afraid I would rip it off.

"On behalf of our Nation, and her majesty the Queen, I would like to say welcome to Australia."

Breathe...

I stared at the letter for a long time, unable to utter a single word. Tears made their way down the bridge of my nose and onto the parchment, marking the last words and erasing the statement that ended my dad's life as a Chilean, and began mine as an Australian. This very letter, evidence of a journey made, the beginning of a new era and giving way to an unknown future. Through unimaginable sacrifice, my father completed the impossible with full awareness he would never again see the life which made him who he was.

"I had no idea," I said through tears, facing my grandma and seeing my agony reflected in her features. I rested my head on my grandma's shoulder as she wrapped her arm around me, providing a comforting presence.

"Now you know the whole story. You know why you are who you are, and now you have found your way home again."

"I miss him so much," I cried.

"Me too, mi amor, me too."

Later that night, unable to sleep, I decided to go for a paddle in the bay. With no wind and a full moon, I couldn't think of a more calming place to be. As I paddled out from shore I glided along the water, breaking its glassy surface which reflected the moonlight so well, I hadn't gone very far before jumping over board into the ocean and swimming as far down as I could, the cool water soaking me to the bone.

Closing my eyes, I floated just under the surface, listening to the silence surrounding me as I let myself go with the movement of the water. Swaying back and forth with the gentle surge of the ocean, I tried to relax. As I entered a state of semi-stasis, my mind returned to my father. Like a flood, I was inundated with thoughts of his story, some through my experience with him: Feeling his touch, hearing his voice, watching him go about his day. This, along with newly discovered elements of his past, finally giving a greater understanding of the man I thought I knew.

Like all stories of the ones we loved, we only occupied a small segment in their life. No matter how much we cared about that person, we must remember they too had their own story, their own memories to build and to share. Stories and memories shared together were also precious, and were in no way less important than any other. Our very presence had formed a part of who they were, and their involvement created the person you were today.

My father was my greatest love. His life was reflected in my day-to-day actions. In the way I behaved, the words I used, the perspective I had on the world. His lessons helped me grow as a person. Passions passed down into my open arms. Although I only made up a small part of his story, he made up most of mine. But now it was time for that story to end.

I returned to the surface. My lungs filled with fresh air as I felt a weight fall off me, washed away by the water and taken out to sea. The burden of guilt: Of my father's death, my decisions since his passing, and the mistakes made to arrive at this point faded away. For the first time in years, I was filled with an unrelenting sense that I was loved. I could feel his presence, watching over me and waiting for us to be together again.

Breathe.

Free from the shackles of despair of my father's passing, I could now fully appreciate my time here. Boris and Rodrigo became constants in my life, taking turns to show me what they knew, what they loved, and providing a holistic view to life growing up in this stunning country.

With Boris it was all outdoor sports. Twenty-four and encumbered by an adventurous spirit, life was only as fast as his surfboard would take him. When we were not surfing, we explored the countryside on horseback, via hiking or by navigating the ever-turning roads on our longboards. The days with Boris went by with lightning speed, each day faster than the previous. How we felt dictated what we did, and when the surf was poor, the mountains were an obvious alternate.

There was so much adventure to be had. With the snow-capped Andes Mountains, a mere three hours away, we honed in our skills as snowboarders and climbers. Camping in the foothills, I revelled in the freezing, mineral-laden waters of glacial lakes, revitalising my muscles for another day of pushing my body to its limit.

It felt like an action movie, each day higher, faster, harder, pushing my body further than I had ever before. A small-town boy from a small farming family, Boris had everything he could ever want, hidden from obscurity and the Western World. His skill was implausible and given the opportunity, he could go pro.

As for Rodrigo, it was slower, a little more refined. Barbeques with the best cuts of meat Chile provided accompanied by an appetiser of good conversation, the only thing homelier were the weekend visits to his family's mountain lodge in the Lake District of the south. Without invitation, Rodrigo frequently showed himself into my grandma's house, immediately putting on the kettle to boil. From there he handed the freshest slices of meat to my grandma with a kiss on the cheek, showing respect to her household and allowing her the opportunity to season the meat in way that you know would make your mouth melt.

Meticulously, as if trying to pass an examination, Rodrigo lifted the kettle off the boil and poured the water through a small strainer filled with freshly roasted coffee beans. Hypnotised, I watched the water cascade through the air, the coffee's aroma relaxing me into a state of submission. With pleasure I took the first cup, sipping the first taste of what was to be another flavour filled night.

"You see, it's all about getting every step right," started Rodrigo. "Everything must come together perfectly. That's what makes the difference. To skip a step is to waste your time. Because it doesn't matter how much you have, it's all about how good it is."

I smiled. Rodrigo just couldn't help himself. He was fascinated by the process and loved how things came together to make something beautiful. In 2016, the coffee laden mountains of Southern Colombia received more rain than normal. This caused the temperatures to rise, springing fruit early and making their flavour bolder. Handpicked, it was washed and transported to a speciality coffee roaster in Concepcion where it was washed again then roasted at the perfect temperature for the exact amount of time. Rodrigo shipped them freshly roasted to his house to grind. Not too thick, causing the water to spill through without catching the flavour, yet not too thin to clog up the machine. Years of experience poured into my cup, full of dedication and meticulous practice to produce a smile and a reason for coming together.

"What are your plans this weekend?" Rodrigo asked.

"No idea. Why, did you have something in mind?"

My eyes widen in excitement as Rodrigo told of a gathering at the family home in Puerto Varas. It was a place I had spoken of many times with Boris. A small German-style town that sat upon a lake, shadowed by the might of Volcan Villarrica, an active volcano that I had the desire to climb.

"The family is coming together to celebrate my granddad's ninetieth birthday," Rodrigo continued, carefully pouring the second cup of coffee and joining me at the table. "It would be great for you to come. You can invite your friend Boris if you like."

It was impossible to hide the joy spreading across my face, a silent smile emerging as I contemplated the details of the trip. It would only take a day to climb the Volcano, giving me plenty of time to attend the birthday celebration and explore the town. Of course, I asked Rodrigo if he didn't mind me sneaking off for a day. After all, he had gone out of his way again to invite me to a unique and intimate experience that celebrated Chilean daily life.

With Rodgo's permission obtained, I relished in an hour-long discussion over the coffee roasting process before showing him out.

Breathe.

"I'm awake", I moaned at my alarm. It was three o'clock in the morning and my eyes refused to open. This lasted a second, as the lights turned on in a blinding haze and a Chilean voice sounded from the living room. "Wake up gringa, we have to go."

Dragging myself out of bed, my legs slowly gained strength as excitement for the day ahead filled me with adrenaline. Knowing it would be an early start, we had our packs and gear waiting at the door, ready to go. This made it easy, and putting on our gear, we walked outside, committing to the mountain.

Rodrigo had lent us his car, and for the next hour we drove in silence, the whisper of night keeping us company as we wound our way up the dirt road to the start of our climb. The wheels crunched on the ice as we arrived. Stepping out, Icicles pierced my lungs as I took my first breath. My face felt hot as blood rushed to my face, only to disappear a moment later as it made its way to my vital organs, causing my cheeks to tingle with a numbing sensation not commonly experienced for a tropical girl.

With one last swig of my hot tea, I put my jacket and pack on, strapped my crampons to my boots and started walking. Map in hand, we made our way up, one foot in front of the other. Walking in crampons felt awkward, having only done it once before on a trip to New Zealand, it took a bit to get used to. Less walking, more stomping in the spikes, far enough apart not to accidently scrape the other leg, yet not too far apart to resemble a constipated duck.

Slowly the terrain turned increasingly more vertical. Our strategy changed. With the mountainside now too steep to walk straight up, we switch-backed left to right, the ice axe on the steep side for balance as we gradually headed towards the summit.

For three hours we continued like this. Only speaking during short water and snack breaks before continuing. Boris had a fire in him, keeping a quick pace, making it hard to keep up. He wouldn't get the better of me, and through a stinging shortness of breath and burning legs, I refused to slow my stride, not willing to show face as the mountain broke me down, one step at a time.

So focused on the task at hand, watching as my crampons spiked into the crunchy ice-snow mix, my fixation had caused the natural beauty of my environment to go unnoticed. Finally, Boris stopped, steadying himself just below the steepest section before the summit. Taking this opportunity to indulge in a moment of much need rest, I turned my gaze horizontal. For a moment I couldn't breathe, not from lack of oxygen, but the sheer magnificence bestowed upon me. It was as if the world had fallen away, mountain peaks in every direction, intertwined by roaring glacial rivers culminating into a great lake in the distance. Above me, the plume of sulfuric steam rose from the peak of our volcano, as if a lord was smoking a cigar in satisfaction as he perused his domain, asserting his dominance of the region.

"I think we should rope up," Boris stated.

I agreed, and tying into the opposite end of the rope, spaced myself back to avoid any slack. It was a small consolation, but if one of us fell, the assurance that we were tied into the other person gave me a safe confidence to keeping going.

No longer were we walking side to side, but attacking the top section straight on, using both hands and feet to climb. Our toe spikes thrusted into the ice, and stepping up, our ice axes did the same. A bit like a monkey climbing a tree, it was a repetitive yet effective motion, and within an hour we crested the top.

Elated, we held hands as we continued towards the centre of the volcano. Sulphuric plumes erupted from the hole in the centre, and being careful not to get too close, we inched forward, trying to see as much into the void as possible. It would've been a surreal moment if not for the intense smell of the billowing smoke intruding my nostrils. Within minutes in became unbearable and I happily receded.

Fog set in as we began our journey back down, moving with gravity as we descended toward a warm home. It took an hour to traverse the steep summit ridge around to the open slope, opening up to a runway all the way to the bottom.

"Woohoo!" Boris exclaimed.

"What is it?"

Boris sat down and removed his crampons, signalling for me to do the same. Blindly, I followed his lead, wondering what on earth was going on. As instructed, I wrapped them up being careful to cover the spikes and placed them in my backpack.

"Now take the plastic square in your bag and clip it between your legs and onto your harness." Boris instructed. I did as he said, starting to catch on but doubting the craziness of what I imagined he was about to propose.

"So, we are going to slide all the way down the mountain on our…how do you say…bums. Use the ice axe as your brake and rudder, holding it by the top and next to your strong side. Do not let go of the axe, but if you have to stop, just roll over onto it and it will dig into the snow."

It was hard to take him seriously as a huge smile erupted on his face. He had done this before and knew the elation it brought. It made me want to shit myself. I didn't really have a choice and with a quick wave Boris took off, disappearing into the fog below.

"Okay, Mari, take a deep breath and go!" The motivating thought quickly disappeared as I soar down the icy runway. Water emitted from the corners of my eyes as the freezing wind iced my cheeks. Faster and faster I went, finding it easy to control my direction and balance with the ice axe. Out of nowhere I heard laughter, a giggling laughter of a little girl. It was me, enriched in the pure happiness of the moment. I let my innocent emotions run free as I slid to a stop at the bottom. Picking myself up from the snow, I turned to find Boris looking back up toward the peak and stood next to him, copying his motion as my head tilted towards the sky. In silence, we took in the beauty of our accomplishment, holding hands as we relished the proud moment before jumping in the car and making the hour-long journey back to Rodrigo's family home.

What greeted us was a blur of activity and noise: Aunties passing plates of food, uncles singing old patriotic odes, children screaming as they scampered about the house playing hide and seek. Each one of these individual acts formed one surreal experience, family. Slightly overwhelmed, yet utterly engrossed in the moment, I found myself lured to the commotion, drawn in like a moth to a lamp. So intense, I felt like I wanted to drown myself in the love filling the room, wafting from everyone like a pungent smell. It was in this moment that I realised that the chasms formed in my soul from heartbreak, loss and years of self-neglect had left voids, now able to be filled with the warmth of belonging.

"Would you like some tea? It helps settle the stomach from the barbequed meat."

With gratitude, I accepted the steeping mug in my hands from one of the aunties. Its steam truly did revitalise my senses, and as I slowly sipped the herbal remedy, I was joined at the table by the rest of the family. Few spoke English, and although they tried to translate for those that didn't, it was hard to keep up. I suppose because I was so used to Boris and Rodrigo's ability to communicate, I assumed that the rest of the family would be multilingual as well. This didn't cause me to feel isolated however, as I was amused by the amicable chaos that ensued as plates of food were passed, toasts were made, and conversations erupted.

Tableside indulgence carried on late into the night, as dinner was followed by dessert, which in turn, was followed by drinks. Although offered multiple times, I politely refused in good faith not only to Boedi, but to myself. I had not had a drink since my arrival, and I felt better than ever. No longer did I yearn for the bottom of a glass, yet was filled with laughter as a game of charades began.

The clock continued to tick and before I could blink, it was two o'clock in the morning. Half the table had fallen asleep, and I took this as my cue to go to bed. No sooner had my head hit the pillow, was I pulled into a deep, soundless sleep.

Breathe.

Three months had passed since my arrival in Chile. So long of a journey it was to get to this moment, yet now that it had arrived, I felt as if no time had passed at all. I had grown very close to my newfound family, and it was with a very heavy heart I now had to say goodbye. This time, however, it was more of a 'see you later'.

I was in my room packing when I heard a knock on the door. Naturally thinking it was my grandma returning from the shops, I rushed to give her a hand with the groceries and was surprised to find Rodrigo standing there, a strange smile on his face as he greeted me with his typical English sounding, "Why hello there!"

"Err, come on in," I gestured for him to enter. "What are you doing here?"

"Surprise!" he said cheekily. "I am here to drive you and your grandma to the airport. I thought it would be a nicer goodbye if we were to see you off. My car is more comfortable than the bus anyway."

"Wow. Thank you. You certainly didn't have to." A small part of me was hoping to sneak out. Old habits die hard I suppose, however I was thankful for the kind gesture and accepted it with ease. "My grandma is still at the shops and I don't have to leave for an hour, do you want to grab a coffee?"

"Fantastic!" said Rodrigo enthusiastically. "Let's go to the café around the corner. They have the best Cortados."

Walking the two blocks to the café was a great break from the melancholic mood brought on by the anticipation of leaving. Rodrigo and I carried on as if it were any other day, with nothing to do but find anything and everything to discuss and relish how the neighbourhood came to life at this time of day: Children playing on the street as their mum's bought the groceries, old men sitting in their chairs as they did every day, reading the paper, chatting with one another or just enjoying the crisp morning air.

Although quite different from what happened back home on the Sunshine Coast, people going about their daily business here reminded me of the bustling Mooloolaba Esplanade. Filled with runners, swimmers, and surfers, all being observed from the loud, glass clinking coffee shops and cafes across the street. I've come to love both places, each bringing a level of comfort felt only in one's own home. It was exactly for this reason that leaving made me happy in some ways, and in many others quite sad. "I'm really going to miss this place I reckon," I said as we took our seats on the balcony of the café.

"That's a good thing!" replied Rodrigo, his smile bigger than a Cheshire cat. "It means you must really like this place, and that you will be back."

"Absolutely! I feel like this is a new home for me."

"No. This has always been your home," replied Rodrigo. "You just hadn't discovered it yet. Your dad used to always say, 'The tide comes in, and the tide goes out, but the shore has always been there.'"

The words were so simple, yet the metaphor more profound than I could wrap my head around. My dad was right and liked the tide returning to the shore, I would be back to greet the family I have always had. We finished our coffees and walked back to my grandma's house in silence, enjoying each other's company one last time. "What are you going to do now?" asked Rodrigo.

"I'm going to Fiji. A big storm is going through the Pacific and my mate Boedi thinks it'll create massive swell along the coast, so he bought us a couple of tickets to try and catch some waves."

"Sounds amazing, hope you get some epic rides over there!"

As we reached the front gate of the house, we found my grandma sitting on the front porch, obviously waiting for me to come home so she could say goodbye. To her surprise, Rodrigo was with me and she was delighted when he revealed his intentions to take us to the airport.

Without further hesitation, I finished packing my remaining items and loaded them into the back of Rodrigo's car. The drive to the airport was a joyous one, with Rodrigo and grandma singing along to classic Chilean Cueca songs, which I was thoroughly amused at watching them belt out ballads from the front seats.

The airport was empty when we arrived, and I was able to check in my bags hassle-free. With few minutes to spare, I turned to say my last goodbyes to grandma and Rodrigo. Rodrigo was first and I gave him a hug, embracing him with everything I couldn't say, before turning to my grandma. To my surprise, she was holding a present. "I can't accept that. It's too much. You shouldn't have gone to so much trouble."

"Please, just open it," she said, handing the carefully wrapped gift over to me.

I unwrapped the paper to find a book titled 'Cautiverio Feliz'. Puzzled, I shot my grandma a look of confusion. As I opened the front cover to investigate further, I noticed a note had been written on the first page.

'Mari,
Dijiste que te sientia atrapada, y por eso te lo compre este libro. Hay que leer lo una y otra vez, por que es como la vida, cada dia una sorpresa.'

(Mari,
You told me that you felt trapped, and for that reason, I bought you this book. You must read it time and time again, because it's like life itself, every day a surprise.)

With a single tear of happiness, I said, "*Nos vemos*."
Breathe.

Chapter 7

"Let's go!" yelled Boedi.

Noise vibrated through the bedroom wall as I heard him in the garage attaching the Jet Ski to the back of the car. It was 4am and we were already running late. Ideally, we'd want to be on the road by now. The night before we checked the surf report, only to realise that our previous predictions were wrong. The waves weren't going to be 15 feet, they were going to be 30. The storm off the north coast of Australia had intensified, resulting in more wave energy being created and directed toward Fiji. To be honest, I had never surfed this size before and I was shitting myself. But I couldn't turn this down. It was the opportunity to surf the biggest waves of my life.

"Mari, hurry up," said Boedi coming into the house.

"I'm coming now," I stated, putting on a shirt and grabbing my bag. "Is everything ready?"

"Yeah bro, just waiting on you mate."

We travelled down the coast, Boedi driving faster than he should in an effort to make up lost time. My heart pounding. I was so nervous. In an effort to slow my heart rate, I closed my eyes and tried to breathe slow and purposeful breaths. Was I prepared for this? Did I have a choice? Yes I decided. Of course, I was ready. This would be the greatest day of my life, accomplishing one of my life long surf goals, to surf a wave taller than 25 feet.

"Mari, we need to have a brief chat." Turning down the radio, Boedi turned to me with a serious look. "Are you sure you want to do this? Because if you do, I'm in one hundred percent but you need to be sure. There is no second chance once you drop into a wave. You can't hesitate."

Turning to face him, I saw that he was staring right into my eyes, as if trying to see if there was any doubt in what I was saying. "Yes. I'm in one hundred and ten percent," I declared.

"Okay, then you need to start breathing," he said after what seemed like five minutes. "Relax, focus on relaxing and remember, if you fall, don't try to fight it. Just stay calm and let the wave take you until you are free of its grip."

Boedi had never been so switched on. The relaxed, easy going, no worries kind of guy had been replaced with an Olympic style swim coach who thought we were going to war. I suppose in a way we were. The rest of the drive passed with an intense silence. From time to time I looked over to see Boedi looking straight ahead and it reassured me he was completely focused on the day to come. He had a huge responsibility I suppose, more so than I realised. Yes, technically I was the one who had to surf the wave, but he was my caddie. But this wasn't just a game of golf, he was responsible for someone's life.

We pulled into the carpark at 4:50am. The sun hadn't risen yet, but light was starting to show over the horizon and I could see waves in the distance. They were too far out from shore to truly appreciate their size, but I could feel their power in the air.

Like clockwork, I unstrapped the boards from the roof of the car whilst Boedi unhooked the Jet Ski. Then packing the boards onto the side of the Jet Ski, I laid the wetsuits and life jackets on the strip of grass next to the boat ramp and helped him push the Jet Ski off the trailer and into the water. The process was well-rehearsed and went without complications, easing my pre-performance nerves and giving me confidence in our ability to work together as a team.

Tying the Jet Ski to the jetty, I hopped onto the strip of grass next to the boat ramp and began my warmup stretches. It was vital to always stretch before a surf, no matter how big it was. Partly therapeutic, the rhythm of the movement helped me focus. The other part just common sense as it loosened my muscles in preparation for the paddling ahead.

"I think we will ride out wide to get a good look at what we are dealing with," Boedi proclaimed officially. "It's hard to see what the wave is doing from here. I think it is peeling off the point, but I want to make sure it doesn't change all of a sudden, and I want to see how deep the reef is. It doesn't look like anyone else is out. Waves to yourself! How good is that?"

Reading his facial expression, it was impossible to tell if he was being a smartarse or sincere. It was hard to tell a lot today, and feeling my snooping eyes, he turned to face me. "It'll be great, and I think you have an audience."

My gaze followed his finger towards the point where a small group of people had gathered to watch the waves, as if daring someone to try and surf them. "Well, here's to putting on a good show," I remarked cheekily. "Which side is my best side?" I broke into a pose and shot Boedi a wink, hoping to lighten the atmosphere and pretending to flirt. Okay, I was definitely flirting as well.

We mounted the Jet Ski and took off. The topography of the sea floor in this area is what created waves so big. Similar to Nazare, Portugal, there was a canyon which ran perpendicular to the shore. As the ocean swell approached the shore, the wave energy was free to flow through the canyon, uninhibited by a rising shoreline, finally hitting the canyon wall and surging upwards, creating unexpectedly massive waves. With the right conditions it was possible to ride these waves. Whether or not you came out of it in one piece was another story.

Excitement started to grow as we approached the point. The waves were now visible, forming perfect barrels and peeling from just off of the point. The lighthouse was still beaming, making me feel more in the spotlight than ever.

"The report was correct. It's got to be 30 feet at least!" Boedi yelled back to me. Silent, I tried to focus. By studying the waves, I could see that the water was being sucked up hard, causing it to barrel quickly and slamming back on to the surface with the power of a ten-tonne truck. "The reef is shallow! Look at the water. I'm going to have to tow you onto the wave from further back to ensure we gain enough speed."

Boedi slowed down the Jet Ski as we approached the outside of the set. Looking at it from this angle, it was easy to see right into the barrelling wave. A spectacular view, it forced me to contemplate every decision which had led me to this precise moment. In the midst of the craziness which currently surrounded me, something diverted my attention to look up at the cliff towards the people standing and watching. They were mostly a blur from this distance, but I noticed one guy off to the side, standing by himself. He wasn't watching the waves, but looking at me, and I could feel his pride. The pride of an unknown stranger on the cliff.

"Are you ready?" Boedi asked, snapping me back to reality. "It's time to show me what you're made of." With ease, I grabbed my board and slid off the Jet Ski, slipping my feet into the straps before sitting back in the water like a wakeboarder. Boedi gently dragged me to the starting spot where we waited, watching the horizon, analysing the approaching swell in order to choose the perfect wave. Picking the correct wave was vital, as it could be the difference between life and death. All of a sudden I saw it, rising out the ocean like a monster who had been bitten on the backside.

"Here we go!"

Boedi gunned it, looking to position himself in the perfect spot at the right time so I could swing out to exactly where I needed to be. The surface was bumpy and I couldn't avoid the bullet like sting of water spraying into my face. The wave under my feet began to rise and I let go of the rope, angling my board to line up with the perfect path I believed would see me to survive this experience.

Dropping in at an extreme pace, I was forced to grab the outside rail of my board to redirect left. Deeper and deeper into the wave I went, struggling to keep up as the mass of water encircled me. Out of reflex, I let go of the rail and turned my board back down the wave to avoid being sucked up and thrown over. This seemed to work, maintaining my position on the wave as I cruised down the line. My heart was pounding and my throat felt constricted as I tried to take long controlled breaths.

The water in front of me began to close in like a curtain falling over me and the bullet like spray was now attacking from behind, pelting the back of my exposed calves, each one distracting me from my goal; to make it out of the tube. My board began to vibrate and I started to lose control as the bumps grew bigger. Noting the precarious situation I now faced, I jumped off the board and bomb dived the water, hoping to get deep enough so as to not get thrown over the falls. It didn't work. Have you ever had a very large person lift you above their head and slam you against the ground? Me either, but I could almost guarantee that it was not at all dissimilar from what I was about to feel any second now...

The pressure was unimaginable and I could feel as water was pushed into my mouth, the salt searing my throat as it made its way down my windpipe. Desperately, I tried to relax in order to conserve oxygen and cover my head to avoid hitting it on the reef. To my relief I didn't reach it and although in pain, was altogether okay. Once breaching the surface all I wanted to do was lay there, but with my body convulsing in an effort to expel the water I had swallowed and knowing I was in direct line of the next big wave, I had no choice but to harden the fuck up and deal with my current situation as best I could.

My board was miraculously still intact and I swam to it with haste. All I could think about was getting out of the way of the next wave. Continuing to dry heave, I climbed onto my board and paddled away from the dump zone and into open water. The roaring of a motor filled the air and I looked up from my vomit session to see Boedi zipping in my direction. He reached me, turning the Jet Ski and extending his hand to grab my arm, pulling me onto the boogie board that was attached to the back. We took off, narrowly avoiding a collision with the next wave.

"Massive stack mate! You almost had it too."

"I want to go again," I replied, overcome by adrenaline and knowing that I could make it.

"Are you sure? You don't have to go, you have proven yourself heaps already."

"C'mon, let's do it." I jumped back onto the Jet Ski and wrapped one arm around Boedi, keeping the other around my board. As we travelled back to the line-up, I replayed the last wave over and over again in my head, trying to find anything I could adjust to make myself go faster. On the initial take off, I didn't realise that I would have to adjust. That extra half a second slowed me down, but if I automatically went more direct this time and not grab the rail, I should be able to make it. Armed with this newfound knowledge, I smiled to myself as I realised that I could actually do this.

We arrived back behind the waves. With adrenaline coursing through my veins, I closed my eyes again and focused on slowing down my breath. In two seconds, out five seconds, that was my rule. It worked and within a minute I was calm and focused. I sat there waiting, and waiting. An hour went by, then another, the whole time watching, studying the waves, none of which made me feel confident that I would succeed or survive. When analysing the approaching waves, you never focused on the first one you see. Generally, sets came in groups of four waves. The first wave was never the biggest and more often than not, the worst quality. If you caught it and fell, you could expect three bigger waves to come down on you.

If the next wave was bigger, you'd be able to see it on the far side of the nearest wave, sneaking a peak like an annoying neighbourhood kid looking over your fence to see what you were doing. This was the wave I got most excited about, taking note of its ridge as it formed over the horizon. If the entire ridge was of equal height, then the wave would crash all at once and you might as well go drown yourself. If the ridge was highest at one point, receding down the line, then you were in luck.

Shivering, I'd been in the water for three hours. Even in the tropics, too much time sitting in the water can make you hypothermic. After paddling around for a few minutes to get my blood to circulate I stopped, suddenly frozen, not by the temperature of the water but by what appeared in the corner of my eye.

On the horizon, I saw the water start to ascend. Hard to see from this distance but my intuition told me this was going to form a monstrous wave. Waiting patiently, I sat still on my board, not wanting to act prematurely. Slowly, it approached, appearing slightly straight but with hope that it would rise off of the point and peel away to form a perfect tube.

"Are you gonna to go for it, Mari?" questioned Boedi, of whom I had completely forgotten was sitting near me. Deciding that now was the time to act, to put it all on the table as one might say, I nodded to answer.

"Okay, grab a hold of the rope."

Refusing to take my eyes off of the wave, I laid back in the water, rope in hand and noticed the wave was going to hit the point at more of an angle. It was hard to read, but I believed this would cause it to open up even more. It was getting closer now and Boedi gradually increased his speed as I popped up to my feet. "Take me closer to the cliff! I need to be closer!"

It was vital to trust your partner, and without hesitation Boedi gunned it toward the point. I readjusted my body for better balance and to be in as much control as I could. The Jet Ski whipped around as we arrived at the point, the wave rising behind. Launching forward to match its speed, I let go of the rope and saw Boedi turn off, getting to safety and preparing to rescue me if needed.

Lifted higher and higher as the wave started to take shape around the point. Concentrating on the situation in front of me and analysing the water, I picked my line of descent, keeping in mind that if the wave pulled hard, I must resist the urge to grab the outside rail, instead pulling my arm back and bending the elbow to point my hand forward. If I wasn't so focused on keeping balanced, I would have laughed at my stance as I looked like a Master Yoda, ready to strike at any moment.

Faster and faster I soared down the face, my eyes fixed on the tunnel forming as the wave began to barrel. There was no need to try and slow down to get inside as it was hard enough to keep up. Trying to gain more speed, I pressed heavy on the front of the board, feeling the tunnel getting smaller as I raced along the wall. Ducking slightly, I turned my board enough to make me face the opening and then grabbed the rail as the water became less steep. Reaching my left hand out in front of me, I held my breath, unintentionally of course, but in anticipation of successfully riding the greatest wave I had ever ridden. Poof! Just like that I was spat out of the end of the tube in victory. Taking a much-needed deep breath, I rose from my stance and stood up straight on my board to ride over the small lip of the wave to the safety of the other side.

"Ahhhhhhh!!! OMG! OMG! Holy fuck!" Clearly lost for appropriate words, I raised my hands in the air only to bring them straight back down, beating the water like a drum. I was so ecstatic that I couldn't control myself.

"YEEEEEEEEEEEWWW!" screamed Boedi, jumping off the Jet Ski and landing next to me in a massive splash.

It was by far the best day of my life. After everything that has happened, I never imagined I'd be here.

Although wet and covered in salt water, I noticed the tears of joy rolling down my face as I hugged Boedi. From behind me I suddenly heard a dull raw and turned to see that the crowd on top of the point were all yelling and cheering. I'd completely forgotten that they were there. Stuck in concentration all else had fallen away. Now I could see them and they saw me and I was filled with such emotion that I punched the air again. "Yeeeeewwwww!" I yelled at the top of my lungs.

Cameras, videographers, phone lights, the whole world was pointed at me, watching. Ignoring them as best I could, my eyes searched for one person in particular; he who previously gave me a sense of self familiarity. Scanning the point right to left, I finally saw him or rather what was left as he disappeared behind the hill, as if a ghost, seemingly satisfied with what he had seen without the need to stay and cheer. "I'm ready to go in," I said to Boedi, jumping on the back of the Jet Ski. "Let's go."

Twenty minutes disappeared as we cruised back to the beach, taking our time to enjoy the water and dwell on the events of the day. I lied my head on Boedi's back, holding tight around his waist and staring out towards the water. Slowly, exhaustion took me and with one last look I witnessed dolphins breaching the water's surface in the distance, playfully enjoying the gift that they called home. They were true creatures of the sea.

"Hey wake up. We're here. There's people that want to see you."

"Ehh. Really? Who?"

"Everyone!"

Groggy and still in the depths of sleep, I blinked open my eyes. Looking up I could see a large crowd waiting on the shore. It reminded me of how winners of surf contests were greeted by a roaring crowd as they exited the water, and although I hadn't won anything in that moment, it felt like the world was mine.

Overwhelmed and unsure how to act, I punched my fist in the air, instantly feeling like an idiot and probably appearing like a tosser who thought she was better than everyone else. As Boedi pulled the Jet Ski against the jetty, I was inundated with pats on the back and arm squeezes as I tried to disembark. Never did I expect an audience, although I didn't think I would have been prepared even if I had anticipated this. Flash, Flash, Click. Cameras were going off everywhere and I tried to push through the crowd, but they formed around me, shooting question after question. It all hit me in a blur, overwhelming me. "Can we get out of here please?"

Without question, Boedi made some space and thanked everyone for their support, backing up slowly to open the car door for me to get in. "I'll drop you back at the house. You can change and rest and I'll come back for the Jet Ski."

"Thank you."

It was impossible to fall back asleep, still exhilarated by the day, adrenaline gone but a deep sense of satisfaction remaining. Boedi was the same and neither of us said a word to each other until we arrived at our driveway. "Don't worry about the boards, I'll get them later. I'll be back in about an hour."

I got out of the ute and walked into the house. Instead of rushing to a hot shower as one might expect, I turned to the coffee machine, just wanting to relax on the veranda with a hot drink and have a moment to myself. Taking off my wetsuit was a struggle in itself, but after five minutes I headed out the back and sat on one of the white wicker chairs, crossing my legs and wrapping a blanket around me. Warmth came over me as I sipped my steaming cuppa, slurping with joy as I stared out to sea. There were all forms of meditation; those whom practiced in a religious way, those whom did meditative yoga, and those whom practiced things they enjoyed. This was one of my forms of meditation; staring out to the ocean, wrapped up in comfort and sipping my favourite coffee. Contradictory to the nature of caffeine, it brought me calm and allowed me to think clearly. Soon enough I was interrupted by the screech and bang of the front screen door as it opened and closed. The noise startled me and looking down at my watch, I realised I must have been sitting here for an hour. To my surprise, there was no more coffee in my cup.

"Mari?"

"Out the back!" I yelled back, not even considering moving.

"Oh, there you are," Boedi stated, poking his head out of the back door. "I'm keen for dinner. I was told of this sick café in town that has the best fish tacos. Wanna go?" It was then I realised I hadn't eaten all day. "Yeah, probably should eat something and fish tacos sound wicked. Let me shower quickly and get dressed."

We pull into the carpark to what looked like a village hut. Big and square with a veranda wrapping around all four sides, it resembled a Polynesian version of a Queenslander and overlooked the ocean on the opposite side of the point from which were earlier today.

The café welcomed you with wooden tables and the smell of fried fish, opening to a sitting area at the back and providing a great view of the sea. A band was playing acoustic guitars in the corner, entertaining the crowd with covers of Xavier Rudd and Jack Johnson and the entire place was lit with string lights shining on a room full of tourists, surfers, and locals alike. We found a spot in the back corner and before even having settled into our seats, a young Fijian girl approached with menus. "Hello, how are you? Would you like anything to drink?"

Boedi stared at me, waiting to see if I had truly changed. This was the first chance he has had to see if Chile had the effect he'd hoped for. "Just a coffee please," I responded politely, looking up at the girl. "OMG! You're that chick from the wave, right?"

"Yeah, that's me," I said softly, feeling slightly embarrassed.

"I'll take a coffee as well please," chimed in Boedi, shooting me a wink and smiling out of the corner of his mouth.

"No worries. This one's on the house. You deserve it."

She turned and ran off to place the order, being sure to tell everyone she could that I was here. Watching her depart, I ignored Boedi has he made a smartass remark about me being famous, but he continued with sincere advice that the attention should only remind me that I should never try and seek the limelight. Today's accomplishment wasn't really about me. That waitress looked up to me and it was not something to snob off. It could inspire her to do great things herself one day.

"Yeah, I suppose you're right," I said as the girl returned, two coffees held in front of her and a smile larger than life on her face. "So I just spoke with the kitchen, they said you can have whatever you want tonight, for free."

"No, you don't have to do that. We are happy to pay. We only want some fish tacos. We've heard you guys have the best in town."

"Fish tacos coming up!" squeaked the waitress and with a giggle, she hopped off toward the kitchen once more.

I was not used to this much notice and could feel myself retreating inwardly from the situation. Taking to heart what Boedi had said, I smiled in an effort to hide how I truly felt. Who was I to be rude? And if it made this young girls' day, then there was no harm done. With any luck I won't draw further attention to myself.

"Boeds, I want to say thank you."

Confusion filled his face as he tried to figure out why I would be thanking him on a day like today. Emphasising my gratitude, I repeated my thanks, even more sincere this time and explaining that I was forever in his debt for bringing me back from a dark place, for Chile, for showing unmoved support, for everything. It meant more than I could ever put into words.

"It's fine," Boedi interrupted. "I would do it again if it meant having you here, eating fish tacos on a breezy night in Fiji. Don't sweat it Mari."

Trying my hardest to hold back tears I took a deep breath and nodded my head in acceptance as our mugs clink together. Boedi wasn't one for getting emotional, and although he didn't say much, I knew the words came with a lot of weight and were spoken from the heart.

We took a drink in silence, looking at each other from across the table. How could I ever let him out of my life? The most reliable person I had ever met, never to abandon me when I needed him most, but to carry me and put forth all his effort to bring me back from a place of no return. To help me find my way, from where I have come to where I was going. "I'm just going to go to the…"

"Hi, are you Mariela Sepulveda?"

Out of nowhere we were confronted by a tall blonde girl, tanned skin and speaking with an American accent. Without invitation she sat down, leaning down to grab something out of her bag. Boedi shot me a quizzical look, only to return the same expression. Whatever this was, I hope it wasn't an autograph or interview or something.

"I'm Bethany. I work for Swell Surf Boards. We saw you today and were very impressed."

"I didn't know you guys were watching," I said, slightly confused.

"Are you kidding me?" she interrupted again, dragging out the last word in a southern Californian drawl. I was starting to get annoyed, and hoped she could get to the point sooner rather than later. "Absolutely! I always come out here when there's big swell. That's when we see amazing things happen like today."

"Well thank you again, is there anything I can help you with? I don't want to be rude, it's just we were having a private dinner." I had never felt more awkward and tried not to look at Boedi. Out of corner of my eye I could see him smiling and knew he found this amusing. Without making any noise, I tried to stomp on his foot.

"Well, I'll cut to the chase," she said, obviously aware that she was making the situation weird. "Have you ever heard of the Swell Classic at Spooky Beach? Well, we want you to go," she said, finally revealing a bunch of papers from her bag. "Fully sponsored and representing Swell Surf Boards. What do you think?"

"OMG, you're shitting me! I mean, are you serious?"

"Absolutely, all you have to do is sign here, and we will look after the rest. If you do well in the comp, we can talk about full representation."

Fighting to keep tears at bay, the overwhelming feeling of joy came over me as a contract was placed on the table. In bold print atop the front page was my name, being asked to represent a surf company and to compete in a pro event. This had to be a dream. This couldn't be real. "I don't know what to say."

"Don't say anything, you've earned it," Bethany said standing up. "I will call you in a week, and we can go over the details of the contest. Bye, Bye." And with that, she walked away, leaving me alone once again with Boedi.

"Can you believe this? I don't think this day can get any better."

"Don't count your chickens before they hatch," Boedi advised. He was right. They were by far the best fish tacos I had ever eaten.

The following week, Boedi and I returned to Australia, I moved out of my place and into Boedi's. That Bethany chick called me and we went over the details of the competition and discussed how I was to represent the company. God I hated the way she talked, but if life kept going the way it was, she could speak any way she bloody liked.

Because I am representing Swell, I had to surf using their gear. Within a week I received four brand new boards: Two short boards, one fish, and a mini mal, all branded of course with the Swell logo on both sides. It seemed they really wanted as much publicity as possible. Having quit my job, I borrowed enough money from Boedi to survive until after the comp, at which point I would have to find out what people called a 'career', whatever the hell that meant. The idea of it terrified me, but I promised Boedi that I would be open to the idea if this competition didn't lead anywhere lucrative.

In the meantime, I had to train. If I wanted a shot at anything, I didn't want my lack of preparation to be the reason for my failure. Like clockwork, I woke up every day at 5am and headed to the beach. If the surf was good, I surfed using the new boards, hoping to be as familiar as possible with how they rode, practicing again and again, trying to perfect all of the moves I knew. It made sense to me that by perfecting familiar tricks, I would have more success than trying something new in an effort to impress the judges.

When the waves were absent, I paddled and rock ran; two essentials for building strength and breath. First I paddled, heading out from the Alex Bluff and making a return trip to Old Woman Island, a distance of five kilometres each way. Always mixing it up, I first paddled on my knees then my stomach, applying long strong strokes followed by quick, short paddles. One thing never changed. I never stopped.

Drying off and loading the board on the car, I drove thirty minutes up the coast to Noosa. It's clear, smooth tropical waters attracted a lot of people on the weekends, however during the week it remained deserted. A welcoming place to train, I swam to the middle of Tea Tree Bay and dove down to a rock I'd placed previously. From there, I lifted it into my arms and walked as far as I could along the sea floor before resurfacing for one long breath, repeating this process for an hour straight. By the end of each session, I was exhausted and literally out of breath. The unrelenting training regime didn't deter me, repeating this every day for a month until two days prior the contest. Never had I been in such great shape. Nor had I felt more confident. "I think I am ready," I said to Boedi coming home from my last training session. "I think I may have a shot."

"Well, if anyone has a shot, it's you. You have been training like an Olympian. I've never seen you so prepared."

The day before the contest was a mad house. More out of nerves than anything, I arrived early, around six in the morning. Everything was already underway. TV stations were setting up, the food trucks were lighting up their kitchens, and some spectators looking for the best seat in the house were already setting up their chairs and blankets, weighing them down with eskies full of hopes for an exciting weekend. Walking around the chaos in an effort to find the sign in area, I quickly became lost in the crowd. In an effort to escape, I pushed past a group of workers, only to run into Bethany.

"Heeeey! There you are Mari. I was hoping you'd show up soon."

"Yeah nah, I'm here all right. Where do I sign in?"

"Follow me, I'll show you, oh and I want to introduce you to somebody."

Bethany darted off, forcing me to jog in order to keep up. Hoping it was a potential sponsor, I stopped suddenly as we came to a scruffy looking guy. Impossible, I was face to face with the world number one, Kyle Newton. "He-llo," I stammered, extending my hand in a way that says: 'Holy shit, you're Kyle Fuckin Newton.'

"Glad to meet you. I saw a video of your ride in Fiji. Sick drop, you've got some skill. I'm glad I'm only judging today, otherwise I'd have some real competition out there."

"Thank you so much. It was a wild ride." I responded, starstruck. "Hopefully one of many."

Kyle walked away to greet some other people and I realised that I was staring, unable to believe that a legend such as Kyle had seen me surf. He saw my big wave. Fully aware that I had been featured in an online article, I didn't realise that news of the wave had spread so high up the ranks of surfing.

Bethany lead me to the registration to sign myself into the contest. The judge explained that I would be one of sixteen girls competing for the top spot, meaning that I had to go through three rounds to place. With so much talent, I was doubtful that I'd win, but did know that with the amount of hard work that was put in to arrive here, I deserved a fair go for a podium seat.

Bethany stayed by my side the entire morning, obviously protecting her investment and ensuring that her sponsored athlete received as much publicity as possible, capitalizing on her gamble to sign me. She introduced me to many people I knew of and a few that I didn't. It was impressive how many connections she had, a clear indication that she'd been doing this for a long time.

The day before the contest was a big social affair. Surfers, photographers, organisers, and fans came from all over the world, being sure to arrive early to have ample time to relax before the fierce ocean battle began. A large marquis was raised on the hill overlooking the beach where the action would begin the following day. The event organisers offered a lunch for the athletes, providing me a great opportunity to meet the people I would be competing against. Sadly, I didn't really know any of them, never much for following the World Surf League, preferring to actually go surfing than to watch someone on TV

The next day, I woke up at 4:30am. It was dark, the sun still hours from rising as I made my way down to the beach to check out the conditions. The cool breeze forced me awake as I breathed what felt like icicles through my nose. New South

Wales was cold this time of year I reminded myself, but it was still early. It would warm up more during the day.

I was not surprised to find other surfers have had the same idea and I took my place beside them on the bluff. Some, still half asleep, were standing alone in silence. Others looked like they were still having a big night, chatting away like it was the middle of a Sunday afternoon barbeque, coffees in hand instead of beers and the smell of egg breakfast sandwiches in place of burgers

The surf looked clean, the ocean just reaching high tide, meaning that in a few hours it would be the perfect conditions for waves. The wind was non-existent, a good indicator that today was going to be hot. It was still too dark to see the waves properly, but in the moonlight, they looked around four feet tall, a good size to pull out all of my practiced tricks and turns.

Seeing all that I could, I made my way to the café for some breakfast, first stopping by Boedi's room to wake him up. With no response to my incessant knocking, I tested the door to find it unlocked and snuck in, trying my hardest to slip through so as to not let in much hallway light. Boedi was lying in bed face down with his back to me, a light snore projecting from the other side of the pillow. Tip toeing through the room, I made my way to the far side of the bed. "Boedi," I whispered loudly. "It's time to get up."

Nothing. Boedi was deep into a snooze without any sign of waking up. Hoping to wake him gently, I snuck into the bed to avoid the shock and jump of waking someone from practically a coma. Slipping under the sheets, I slid over to Boedi and tapped him on the cheek with a finger. "Hey mate, you have to wake up. The contest starts in an hour and a half."

"Mmm, uhmp… Okay," grunted Boedi back, slowly starting to regain consciousness. "Are you in bed with me? I'm naked."

"Well, then… Hello!" I exclaimed, slightly embarrassed, but somewhat unmoved. "Maybe I should just leave you to it."

"Or you could stay, I've heard it helps calm the nerves," Boedi mumbled through his pillow, as if half-heartedly thinking that it could happen. Picking up the pillow under me, I struck him in the side, partly to get him back for saying something like that, but also as a distraction to hide my desires. Focusing on the competition today was my priority and now was not the time to fuck that up. Before getting out of bed, I belted him again, this time on the head.

"I'll meet you in the café," I said, making sure to turn on the lights before exiting. Boedi met me ten minutes later, half-awake and yawning as he took his seat. Slowly adding sugar to his coffee I'd ordered, he stare at it whilst stirring in the sweet start to the day. Before I could say anything, Bethany suddenly rushed over to the table

"I thought I might find you here!" she squealed as she sat down. "You are in the second round today, so you have a while before you need to surf, but you have to be there for the opening ceremony in forty-five minutes."

"No worries, want some vegemite?" I offered, pushing the plate towards her.

"Eww gross," she cringed. "That does not look appetizing at all."

"Nah mate, it's so good! It's pretty much a requirement to eat it daily in Australia." Shooting a smile at Boedi, I crossed my fingers that the joke would work and gain great satisfaction as the American's face cringed to an unfamiliar black and salty paste. Unfortunately, she didn't fall for the trick and turned down the offer. After finishing her piece of toast, she quickly became bored and saying something about needing to check on the event, excused herself with haste. Finished with my scone and coffee, and needing to grab my gear, I also excused myself, telling Boedi to meet me at registration in twenty minutes, before dashing upstairs to grab my wetsuit, short board, and numbered competitor's rash guard. After triple checking to make sure I hadn't forgotten anything, I headed downstairs and made my way over to the crowd gathering at registration.

There were so many people it was ridiculous. 'Is this what all contests are like?' I thought as I tried to break through the crowd of volunteers, photographers, event organisers, sponsors, and whoever else in the world felt like getting in the way. I Pushed my way through and finally found my way to the other competitors, all silently stretching with their game faces on.

I found a change area and quickly put on my wetsuit and rash guard. I was nervous and without thinking I put on the rash guard backwards. Wrestling it off to turn it around, the announcer began declaring the line-up over the loud speakers. "Round one: Rose, Deborah, Liz, Becks. Round two: Emma, Sarah, Beth, Lorraine. Round three: Allanah, Jane, Leslie, Patty. The top surfer from each round will move on to the finals rounds tomorrow."

"What," I gasped. "They never announced my name."

Confused and wanting answers, I dashed out of the changing area and made my way to the judge's panel. "Hi. I'm Mari. I'm supposed to be competing today, you never announced my name," I panted.

"The rest of your heat never showed up, so you get a free pass into tomorrow's rounds. Unfortunately, the rules state that there can't be more than four competitors at a time," informs the head judge. "Most people would be stoked to get a free chance for a medal. Congratulations."

Devastated as I wanted to earn my place by out surfing the others. I didn't want to spectate, but rather to be a part of it, cheering on the other girls as a member of the line-up, not sitting out only to feel like any medal I win tomorrow, if I win any at all, would be because I had the advantage today.

"When do you go?" asked Boedi as he finds me in the line for the change room to take my wetsuit back off.

"I don't, I got a pass."

"Sweet!" Boedi exclaimed.

"Yeah, I really want to surf though. Do you think they will care if I sneak off for a surf up the beach?"

"Not if they don't see us," whispered Boedi in my ear. He leaned back and gave me a wink. "I heard the other side of the point is rippin'."

Done. Without further hesitation, I exited the line and followed Boedi to his car. To avoid suspicion, I left my board where it was locked up in the competitors' tent and borrowed one that Boedi had brought. We drove down the road, and hoping that no one had seen us, parked along the side of a track that lead down the north side of the point.

With everyone at the contest, we were ecstatic to find no one in the water. There was only one guy on the far side of the beach sitting down and watching the waves. We quickly untied our boards from the roof and I left Boedi to change into his wetty as I made my way up a track to the end of the point, opting to jump out from there rather than paddle all the way from the beach.

Standing on a large rock, I waited for the precise moment to jump. Watching as the waves the came in, I was aware that if I timed it wrong, I'd be swept into the rocks, placing me in a precarious situation. The last wave of the set came in, approaching in a white fury as it cleared everything out of its way. As if in slow motion I watched as it got closer and bending my knees like a spring, launched myself forward, extending my board out in front of me.

Landing on the back side of the white water, I immediately paddled away from the rocks as fast as I could before the next set came in. Finally, after what seemed like forever, I made it clear to the far side of the breaking waves, finding the outgoing current that carried me the rest of the way to the break point. The water was cool and I jumped off my board to escape the heat of the now risen sun. Remerging to the fresh smell of salt filled air, I could see Boedi swimming out to join me.

"Are you ready for some real competition? It's picking up to five feet. I reckon I can get tube first!"

"Bring it on Champion! Here comes the first set!"

With no one around, I easily found the perfect position to catch the lip of the wave. The wave wrapped hard around the point and the water rose quickly, walling steeply from behind. It lifted me into the air fast, and with one final stroke, I angled my board to face my chosen line down the wave. With the board dropping down below me, it was easy to get on my feet and in position, squatting down and extending my right arm to drag my hand along the wall of water beginning to surround me.

The wave was too steep and with a thruster fin set up on the board, I raced way ahead of the position I needed to be in. No tube ride, but still an epic wave, I turned sharply off the top and re-angled my board down the wave. It held and with no sign of getting slower, I continued to climb and fall on the wave, performing turns on the bottom and top similar to a snow boarder cruising down a long hill. Finally, halfway back to the beach, the wave dissipated and I performed one last bottom turn before launching myself off the top of the wave like a superhero and diving into the water on the other side.

Using my board to help me float, I relaxed in the coolness of the sea and relived the memory of the magnificent wave just ridden. After several minutes of bliss, I looked up towards the beach and noticed the guy from before, now standing with his hand above his eyes to protect from the glare of the sun as he looked out toward me. Recognising him immediately as the same guy from Fiji, he was the one that walked away from the cliff after my big wave. Was he a big-time surfer guy? What was he doing here? Was he here for the contest? Was he stalking me? He seemed so familiar, yet I couldn't make out his face.

"Hey!" I yelled, waving my arms to grab his attention. He didn't respond but continued to watch. After about twenty seconds, he lowered his arm and against my wishful thinking, turned away, walking from the beach and leaving me once again.

"Hey!" I yelled even louder. He didn't respond, and as if disappearing all together, walked out of view behind the coastal bushes.

"Yeeeewww!"

Splash. Boedi bomb dove next to me. He came up for air and squirted water from his mouth into my face. Laughing, he questioned my interaction with the man on the beach.

"I swear I saw him on the top of the cliff in Fiji and again months ago at Alex Beach. It's like *deja vu*. It's doing my head in."

"It's probably just your mind playing tricks on you. These waves are epic! What are you waiting for?"

And with that, Boedi and I started paddling back out, racing each other for position and letting our competitive spirits fly. Back in the line-up, Boedi had position. He took off, got caught too steep and fell. I saw his board fly up into the air and cringed as I witnessed the massive break in the middle. Snapped board!

For a moment, my heart stopped and adrenaline kicked in. Scanning the water, I waited for the signal to go after him. Fifteen seconds later, he re-emerged and as quickly as he could swims over to the safety of the rocks. Giving me the thumbs up to indicate that he was okay, I prepared to catch a wave for myself, hopefully better than Boedi.

In the same exact fashion as my previous wave, I popped up without issue and picked my line. Angled more laterally, I was able to maintain a slower speed down the wall as it folded over my head. I was in the tube! Time to focus, the wave was closing fast and I needed more speed. I leaned forward onto the front of the board and took my hand out of the wave, pointing it out in front of me in order to get a heavier centre of gravity. It worked and I soared forward. Seeing an opening, I turned left to pop out of the wave before it closed on top of me.

Still not fast enough. The wave closed so close behind me that the whitewash surged forward, taking me and my board into a rush of twisting, turning water. It tossed me around like a shirt in a washing machine. The only thing I could do was cover my head for protection and let the wave do with me what it pleased.

With Boedi out of action and being bashed around like a rag doll myself, I took the hint that the session was over. Not exactly a glorious finish, but a great time and with great results. It was way more than I expected and a million times better than watching other people surf. With success, I was able to re-enter the event unnoticed. It was the last round of the day and everyone was focused on the competitors. Being sure that no one had seen me, I snuck into the competitors'

132

tent and quickly changed out of my wetsuit. 'What a day!' I thought as I pulled my shirt over my head.

Suddenly the judge from earlier came into the tent. He seemed surprised to see me and from the quizzical look on his face, I could tell that he had suspicions for why this was the first time he had run into me since the morning.

"Where have you been?" he asked, "I haven't seen you all day."

"Oh well, since I wasn't in the line-up today, I thought I would enjoy the comp with my mates instead of sitting with strangers in the competitor's booth. Great results!" I said.

Hoping I was right about the great results, I had to use something to sound more convincing. It seemed to have worked, and the judge slipped back out of the tent and out of sight. I re-joined Boedi in front of the podium and looked at the results for the day. All of the expected people had made it through to the medal round tomorrow with no surprise victories.

Whether or not I knew who they were, it didn't change anything, I was here to surf the best for me. If I ended up beating some of the others, well that was just the cherry on top. Bethany joined us and in her usual manner, she seemed more concerned with getting everything organised than enjoying the day.

"We have been invited to the athlete's dinner," she said. "I have already accepted on your behalf. All of the sponsors will be there. Come on, we have to get you something to wear."

"No, we don't. I have clothes you know?"

"Not for this dinner you don't. C'mon, I'm not taking no for an answer," she insisted.

"Fuck sake. Fine." I won't waste time telling you how much I hated looking and trying on clothes. I'll just say it was a terrible ordeal. Bethany got what she wanted and I spent enough money to buy a new board. The final result being me looking like a doll in order to impress people I didn't know.

"Stop complaining. It's just one night. Just remember, if the right people like you, you could get a lot more sponsorship, including from my boss," Bethany reminded me.

We drove to the dinner in silence. Located at the local hotel, the organisers had rented the entire banquet hall. It was way over the top, with white table clothes, silver and ceramic place settings, and fully catered in a buffet style. There was a podium at the back of the room, I assumed so that someone could give a speech or maybe honour the biggest sponsors. Why was any of this necessary? Was it just for show or were the organisers controlled by the event sponsors? Maybe it was all normal and I was just not used to it. Either way, Bethany didn't make it any better.

Clinking metal cutlery, silent chewing, the soft murmur of conversation, a baby crying in the corner gently being shushed by an embarrassed mother. Looking around at the scene that enveloped me, it was evident that I didn't belong here. It felt like I was the ugly duckling, following the same routine as everyone else in the room yet acutely aware that I was not a duck, no matter how hard I tried.

Needing some air, I excused myself and made my way out to the back veranda. The cool night was a refreshing change from the suffocating atmosphere inside. My feet hurt and I kicked off my flats, leaving them in the corner as I made my way to the railing for a better view of the bay below. The breeze was blowing quite consistently, bringing a chill to my spine as it gave me a firm reminder of where I should be.

I couldn't help but think about the day, the best part being the hours spent surfing with Boedi, enjoying the moment, surfing amazing waves and caring about nothing else. For the time, I wasn't in the contest, I was just on a surf trip, lucky enough to get waves to ourselves, something that rarely ever happens. Wasn't that the whole point?

Why was I doing the contest? It doesn't seem like something I would typically do. Was it because I saw it as an opportunity to get sponsored so that I could surf full time and go on awesome trips? But wasn't that what I was doing already, and in abandoning my chance at the contest, I was finding what I was looking for anyway? The more I dwelled on it, the more the contest seemed less like a light at the end of the tunnel and more like a public farce, distracting me from what I really wanted.

"I hope I'm not interrupting."

Jumping out of thoughts, I turned around. It was the competition judge from earlier that almost caught me skipping the contest. Without invitation, he walked over, and joining me on the railing, handed me a glass of clear liquid.

"Thank you very much, but I don't drink."

"It's just water. You're in competition. I'm not going to try and ruin your chances," he responded earnestly.

"Oh, Okay. Cheers!" I said, going along with the scene and taking the glass with delight.

Hoping to break the silence through action and give an excuse to my awkwardness, I took a large drink from the glass. The façade could only last for so long and putting the glass down, I looked out over the bay slowly being swallowed by darkness as the clouds covered the sky.

"You weren't really at the contest today," the judge stated, completely ignoring any attempt at small talk. "I saw you sneak off with that guy of yours. You had your wetty on and surfboards loaded. I saw you surfing the point during my lunch break."

"I…I…um," I stammered. Fuck, busted. I didn't see him at all, least of all I expected to be caught.

"Don't worry. You're not in trouble. You surf really well you know. I reckon you could have won your heat today if you'd been in the first round."

"Really?" I said surprised. "Thank you."

"I could ask why you skipped out, but it seems pretty obvious. I would have done the same thing."

I couldn't really see his face anymore, but I could tell he was looking back at me. It was a face that echoed the thoughts running about my head. 'What's the point?'

"I should probably get back. Err, thanks for the water," I said.

The dinner had finished and everyone was waiting for the speech and sponsor recognition. There was no way I was going to wait around for this, but not wanting to be rude, I whispered to Bethany that I was not feeling well and excused myself outside, before casually making my way to my room. Somehow, the conversation with the judge had eased my mind slightly and with nothing left to do, I went to bed.

It was early, yet I woke up in a great mood. Today was going to be epic. The night's sleep had given me a sense of clarity to my constant back and forth of moral dilemmas. Finally, I knew what I wanted to do and ironically enough, I didn't want to do anything. I was going to go back to the point and I was going to surf the same amazing break as yesterday. Sure, I was giving up on the potential of being sponsored to surf in competitions all over the world, but for the moment, I had everything I needed and I was not going to sacrifice my current happiness to try and achieve something that may never happen. Yes, I've always wanted the freedom to surf full time, but that price is not something I wanted to pay right now.

With my decision made, I took my time getting ready, enjoying the warmth of the shower as it cleansed me of any remaining doubt and reminded me that even without competing, I was still in the best point of my life.

Having dried off, I packed my bag as normal and headed down to the competition tent. Looking around, I found who I was looking for. The judge was talking to the organisers, going over las minute details of the day's events. He saw me approaching and looked up in surprise. Clearly, he would have thought I would be getting ready with the other surfers, but as I drew closer, I could read how his facial expression reflected a sudden realisation as to why I was here.

"Mari, aren't you supposed to be getting ready for your heat?" he said.

"Can I talk to you in private please?" I asked, gesturing my head slightly to indicate a moment of privacy. "I have decided to pull out of the competition," I continued. "Before you say anything, just know that I take this decision seriously and apologise for any inconvenience it may cause."

"I can't say that I'm shocked," admitted the judge. "I kind of got the hint last night. It's a shame though, I think you could have won from what I saw on the water yesterday."

"Well let's just hope the surf is as good today, because I'm going back to the point."

"But no one will be there to see you perform," responded that judge.

"And that's the whole point."

Excusing myself, I found my way through the now gathering crowd to Boedi, who had parked up on the street without a question in mind as to what would be on today's agenda. About to step into his car, I heard a yell from behind me and turned around to see Bethany walking towards me, wearing a very cross expression on her face. "The judge just told me that you quit the contest! Are you crazy?" she yelled

"Look mate, it's just not for me, and it would be a lie to go out there under a false precedent."

"If you leave today, you lose any future sponsorships with us. I hope you know that."

"I understand. That is just something I will have to live with," I said, hopping into the passenger seat and motioning for Boedi to drive. We drove off, leaving Bethany standing there, dumbstruck.

My fingers were crossed in hopes of another day by ourselves on the point. With the finals of the competition underway, I couldn't imagine it being any busier than yesterday. We arrived in the carpark to find an old Subaru, its driver missing and suspected that we may have company in the water. Walking down to the beach, my suspicions were confirmed as I saw the nose of a longboard sticking out at me, being ridden by a local also hoping to have the day to himself.

With hopes of being welcome without ruining his solitude, I paddled out to him behind the break. The waves were smaller today, maybe three feet, but approaching in a more easterly direction, travelling through the entirety of the bay. Riding Boedi's fish surfboard, I was hoping its wider surface would allow me to be carried along these lines as if gliding across the sky. The board was easy to move, caught lots of water yet turned without resistance, allowing me to experience every angle the wave had to offer.

As I arrived at the old man, he greeted me with a nod before turning to prepare for the oncoming set. As if by memory, he hopped onto the first wave and glided forward. Walking up and down his board like a plank in order to reposition himself, he eventually found the sweet spot he needed to get the ride he was hoping for. With the next wave walling up behind me, I followed in his steps, smoothly landing on my feet to cruise down the line.

"Haha!" I laughed aloud, sitting on my board and placing my toes on the front tip. The smile was impossible to wipe from my face as I continued to cruise down the wave, using my wave side hand to keep me balanced. In reaching the bottom of the wave, I jumped back onto my feet and took a deep but sharp turn up before skidding across the top and returning to the bottom for another turn. This movement continued for the rest of the wave before turning over the lip for a long paddle back to the start.

And this is how we went, the old man and I swapping rides in silence, enjoying the solitude as much as each other's company. A small group of people had gathered on the beach, standing and pointing at first before getting out their cameras to take photos. Most likely, they were tourists enjoying the beach and watching the surfers in hopes of trying it themselves one day.

The sun was straight above me, indicating that it must be around noon and at least four hours in the water so far. Exhaustion and dehydration were starting to take their toll, but the adrenaline and good vibes were blocking any thoughts of leaving this glorious place. The old man was feeling it too, and with a lifetime of surf comes experience. He would take the day for what it was, ending on a high note as he paddled back to shore. Waving goodbye, I noticed that Boedi was waving for me to come in.

Curious to request, I began paddling into shore, hoping to milk the last moments for everything they had. Boedi had made his way back to the beach and had begun chatting to the group of people I saw earlier, no longer taking photos or even looking out to sea, but focusing on me as I exited the water. Boedi approached me alongside a sandy haired photographer, smiling from ear to ear as if he knew something that I didn't. "Hey Mari, come and meet Mick!"

"G'day Mick. How are ya mate?" I said, shaking his hand. "Sorry if I don't seem excited to meet you, I'm just bloody tired, but the pleasure is all mine."

"No worries. Completely understandable. You surf really well," he said. "I think we should get a coffee. I'm friends with the judge and he told me that coming here today would be worth missing the contest. I'm happy to say he was one hundred percent correct. I'm the owner of Drift Surf Co. and I think you are exactly the person we are looking to sponsor."

Mick smiled as I stumbled backward in shock. So much for a bloody surf photographer.

"Are you serious?" I asked.

"Absolutely. I want someone that searches for the lifestyle that surfing demonstrates, and the freedom that it dictates. Obvious, you have to be able to rip as well. Now, how about we get that coffee and discuss your future."

Breathe.

Chapter 8

Elated barely describes how I felt. A sponsorship to travel and surf full time. The opportunity to surf everywhere I had ever dreamed, and to discover, to journey, to find answers to questions I had yet to ask. Never had I felt so uninhibited, free for the water to take me.

"Congratulations Mari!"

I turned around to see Boedi walking towards me with two coffees. "Thanks mate," I said, reaching up and grabbing mine.

"You're a champ now, stoked"? asked Boedi, shooting me a cheeky wink as he sat down by my side. He wrapped the blanket around us both to warm us from the cool coastal breeze.

"Yeah nah, more curious I reckon. Curious of what's to come. But yeah, it's goin' to be amazing."

We sat there for a while, I wasn't sure how long to be honest, taking in the warmth of the coffee, watching the waves roll in. Today they had built to seven feet, massive for this time of year, but expected due to the storm blowing out in the pacific.

Feeling the cold, I snuggled into Boedi and tried to steal his warmth. As I laid my head on his shoulder, I felt a connection. Boedi had been the one that had been there through it all. He knew me completely, all of my failings, and what was hoping would be all of my successes or maybe I was just crushing…

"Is there something here?" I asked.

"Yes, and I happen to think she's amazing, although I may go broke, 'cause she's pretty high maintenance, haha!"

"Smartass."

My eyes began to flutter, sleep was coming over me. Suddenly, I heard a woman's scream in the distance.

Muffled by the wind, I ignored it, hoping that whoever that lady was screaming at her child would go away. Looking over I saw that Boedi was fast asleep, before closing my eyes again. I heard another scream, this one more distinct. The woman was yelling for her kid. "Help! My son can't swim. Help!"

My eyes shot open to see an olive-skinned woman with black hair jumping and waving her arms, the scarf around her head falling over her face. In an effort to see who she was screaming for I followed the beach line and noticed a small boy in the water splashing with his arms, showing obvious signs that he couldn't swim, especially not in ocean conditions.

As the rip continued to take him further out to sea, I looked beyond and saw his destination. He was heading straight for the seven-foot dumping waves! Without hesitation, I jumped to my feet and sprinted to the car. Adrenaline was pumping through me, causing my hands to fumble on the straps holding my board to the roof.

"C'mon!" I yell.

After what seems liked an age, I finally got the straps loose and took my board off the car. Turning towards the beach with haste, I didn't pay attention and as my board spun around, it smashed against my passenger mirror.

It was a long way to the surf, having to follow a path down a large hill, but I ran as fast as I could. Breathing hard, I tried to keep one eye on the boy, watching him slowly drift out toward the waves. As if in slow motion, I could see the horror in his face. This only made me go faster, not filled with panic as I might have thought, but of action.

Adrenaline was an amazing thing. Fight or flight, the chemical reaction forcing you to focus and act, whatever that act may be. It allowed you to forego all other emotions in an effort to save oneself or another.

Sprinting towards the shoreline, I took a second to look at the woman as I passed her on the beach. She was in hysterics, her only child I imagined, her everything, slowly drowning in front of her, unable to do anything but watch. Her face said it all, the expression that stated, 'How is this happening?'

Finally reaching the water, I launched myself onto my board, paddling as fast as I could. Twenty metres out, the first white water approached, I duck dove under the wave and upon resurfacing I could see it. Just an arm, anxiously trying to stay afloat, as if the boy himself was reaching for the hand of god. With all adrenaline gone, I panicked.

"Ahhh!!!" I screamed. "I can't lose you! One stroke, two strokes, three, four, five." Breathe.

The secondary swell was fast approaching. On the other side, the boy, slowly slipping into the cold embrace of Neptune's welcome. Out of breath, my chest burned as I paddled as hard as I have ever in my life towards the boy. The swell arrived and with one last stroke, I hurdled over it, using the kinetic energy to launch myself into the air and dove into the water. The boy floated motionless just above the sea floor. As I reached him, I cradled him like a child being carried off to bed before spinning around, placing my feet firmly on the coral and launching towards the surface. Unseen in the saltwater, I could feel myself crying, weeping.

The boy remained motionless as I laid the child on my board. "Oh no! Oh no! Oh no! C'mon, you little shit, breathe!" I tried to give him mouth to mouth, but with the bobbing motion coming from the intensity of the water, it was too difficult.

I slapped him.

I slapped him hard.

"Wake up!!!"

He coughed, spewing saltwater out of his mouth as I turned him on his side, helping him breathe. He began to convulse as he slowly gained consciousness.

"It's all right mate. You'll be all right. Cough it up." I continued to reassure him, although it felt like I was doing it more for my own sake. "You're going to be okay, let's get you back to shore. I want you to hold onto the board, no matter what, okay?"

The boy nodded, acknowledging that he had understood. Turning around to jump on the back of the board, I realise that we had drifted out further to sea. Out of instinct, I pushed the board towards the shore as hard as I could, hoping that it would clear the path of the water smashing down from above. Shoving the board forward, I took the full force of the seven-foot wave... Blackness.

I awoke. My neck hurt beyond belief and I was bleeding from what I suspected or rather hoped was my nose. Underwater, I looked up to the surface and could see my board, the tip in the air as my weight pulled on the leash from the back. The child's legs kicked in the water and I was happy that he had followed my instructions and held onto the board. Knowing he wouldn't survive another wave, I started to swim towards the surface.

'What the fuck?' I thought as I felt my leg jam, allowing me to go no further. Looking down, I was horrified as I realised the entirety of my situation. My foot was stuck in a hole in the coral. I pulled hard, trying to free myself. I pulled again, still nothing. I reached towards the world above, the little boy still kicking hard, obviously in a panic, a panic that I could feel coming about in me.

Blood poured from the cuts as I pulled harder, desperately trying to break my foot out. It wasn't working. My lungs started to convulse. I needed to breathe.

Crack!

"Ahh!!!"

My ankle broke under the pressure of the manic pulling. It didn't work, I was still stuck. The boy had only seconds before he was presented with the same fate as myself, the water moving as the incoming wave sucked it in, building in height and preparing to dump.

All of my senses were on overdrive. My heart beat through my chest, everything was moving slowly, my chest convulsing under the desperate need to reach the surface. With no other choice, I untied the strap holding me to my salvation and the boy to his demise, and watched as the wave crashed, launching the board forward. As four fins cut through water to deliver a boy to the arms of his loving mother, I observed as his legs disappeared from view, leaving me with nothing, and everything.

Silence. Often unheard, I was overcome by it. With it came a sense of calm, of peace, washing over me as the waves washed over the surface of the sea. I thought of my dad. I could feel him.

It was a silence like I have never heard before and it covered me like a blanket, blocking out the reality that was occurring. With it came a clarity, the ability to see more clearly than I have ever in my life, providing me with a reflection of the path that brought me to this moment. It seemed normal, an unexpected welcoming. For some reason, I didn't think of Boedi, or the boy, or getting out alive. I thought of the last thing my father said.

"Once more I think of you, to the last time that you go. I am okay, because I know that the fight is over, and you are at peace. You have gone to the place you belong, and for that I love you.

Take yourself there, let yourself go. You have returned, to the home you have always known."

As I recited these words, he appeared before me, and I realised that he had been with me the entire time: On the beach, in Fiji, at the contest. Now it was my time to join him, to complete our journey together.

Breathe.

Afterword

By Boedi Lusano

G'day Mari,

And here we are, drinking on the beach as if nothing has happened. I brought you a beer, in case you decide to show up.

We spread your ashes in the ocean today, the same way we did when your father passed. It seemed the most appropriate thing to do, and I knew you wouldn't have it any other way.

Is it wrong to feel happy? I thought I would be sad, lonely, or even distraught, but I know that even in your absence I am not alone. I carry you with me always.

You have taught me the greatest lesson of all. Life is a cycle; peace, fury, and once again peace. That is enough for me.

Do one thing for me. When the sea is churning and the waves are rough, go to those in need. Watch over them as I have watched over you and bring them comfort. Tell them everything is going to be okay, and to not be afraid. Guide them to safety so that they may live another day and find peace themselves.

This will be the legacy of Maria Sepulveda, and this is how it begins.

CPSIA information can be obtained
at www.ICGtesting.com
Printed in the USA
LVHW081705310520
657067LV00021B/2677